Suzana Tratnik

Games with Greta
& Other Stories

Translated by Michael Biggins, Tamara Soban, Špela
Bibič, Mojca Šoštarko and Elizabeta Žargi

DALKEY ARCHIVE PRESS

Translated from Slovene by Michael Biggins, Tamara Soban, Špela Bibič, Mojca Šoštarko and Elizabeta Žargi.

The Library of Congress has catalogued this title as LCCN: 2016005094

This book is partially funded by a grant by the Illinois Arts Council, a state agency.
Published in cooperation with the Slovene Writers' Association—Litterae Slovenicae Series.

This work has been published with the support of the Trubar Foundation, located at the Slovene Writers' Association, Ljubljana, Slovenia. This translation has been financially supported by the Slovenian Book Agency.
With the Support of the Creative Europe programme of the European Union.

This project has been funded with support from the European Commission. This publication [communication] reflects the the views only of the author, and the Commission cannot be held responsible for any use which may be made of the information contained herein.

www.dalkeyarchive.com

Victoria, TX / McLean, IL / Dublin

Dalkey Archive Press publications are, in part, made possible through the support of the University of Houston-Victoria and its programs in creative writing, publishing, and translation.

Cover: designed by Heidi Pungartnik

Printed on permanent/durable acid-free paper

Contents

Games with Greta 3

Below Zero 17

Sewing the Princess 28

Key to the Restroom 43

The Subway 50

Letters from a Prisoner 59

Proculin 70

Trips Are Cheaper Now, Too 77

Discretion Guaranteed 89

Letters Without Envelopes 95

The Greenhouse 105

Geographical Positions 116

Something I've Never Understood
   About Taking the Train 122

GAMES WITH GRETA

I first met Greta when I was six, when my parents took me to a big yearly get-together of all our relatives in Vučja Vas. Greta had been adopted by "the English," that's to say, a couple of our relatives who'd lived in England for over twenty years. I found the English aunt and uncle condescending and unkind, though their behavior was always pointedly polite. I only met them a few times in my life, but they invariably talked about the same things, the same people, the same events. They'd describe life in London as if it were almost a fairy tale, the land of milk and honey for capable people, which was obviously what they considered themselves to be too. My parents would listen to them with enthusiasm and awed wonder, and then brag about them for a long time in front of our neighbors.

It was precisely because of the "English" that I didn't at all look forward to the great family reunion; I felt self-conscious in advance about all the gauche things I'd say or do, uncomfortable about the contrite look on the face of the hostess because her soup was too greasy, and downright ashamed of the dilapidated and messy house in Vučja Vas where our entire family would regularly assemble at least once a year and have an uninhibited good time—or so it seemed to me. This time a host of unpleasant feelings descended upon me as soon as we reached the gravel road leading to Vučja Vas, and all because of some people living on a distant island. And so I didn't much care what their adopted child Greta was like, whom the English had acquired since their last visit and whom none of us had yet met.

As a matter of fact, I'd decided beforehand that I wouldn't

like her and that I'd furtively be as mean to her as possible—I'd find some way for her to start repaying me evil in kind. Once we were at war, things would be easier. I wondered nonetheless what her adoptive parents tortured her with. For me, it was English. Come to think of it, everybody hassled me about English. My grandpa was always boasting about his granddaughter who took English classes at the age of six already, and he told me to thank my aunt and uncle in English for the candy they'd bring me, and to speak loud and clear as though I was speaking Slovenian. My previous encounter with "the English" had ended in disaster. As soon as I stood in front of them I couldn't even remember my name, let alone the way I was supposed to address them in English. Their speech sounded absolutely alien and unreal, and in my despair I ended up repeating "thank you" and "please" loud and clear, to show at least my willingness and good manners, since all my knowledge of English had evaporated, and to get out of their clutches as quickly as possible. I got the candy eventually, but because of the humiliation I'd suffered at their hands in front of all my kin, that candy was a source of shame to me, and I feared that the village kids, among whom I'd enjoyed leadership status due to my city origins, would start treating me as an equal.

Greta undoubtedly knew English, and knew it so well she never needed to attend any foreign language classes. I clearly had no advantage there. I just hoped she could speak no Slovenian, which might put her in a predicament in front of the assembled company. Even back then, Greta was a hard nut for me to crack.

That year the English were late to arrive, a circumstance that caused universal, though unvoiced, joy. The greasy soup was quickly all lapped up, the fried chicken picked to the bone and then the bones sucked clean, a thing not done in England; apparently bones there weren't even given to dogs and cats, but thrown out of the window, to the birds. After lunch, the entire family gathered in the yard to dismember the pig slaughtered in the morning, without anyone finding fault with the village women's remarks about how beautiful the fresh meat was with the nerves still quivering in it. I was allowed to watch while my grandma strained the pig blood onto giant iron pans and then inserted them carefully, like some very precious material, into the oven of the red-hot wood stove. I touched the edges of the pans, despite my grandma's constant admonitions that she didn't need my help. She nonetheless wearily let me interfere with her work, and get my hands and arms covered with blood up to the elbows. It would've been great if the English had showed up at that moment to find us children naughtily hugging and caressing each other with bloody hands, just to be bad. Because: "Blood is associated with violence, and violence is bad for children." I think that's what the English aunt had once said. I can't recall why. As far as I was concerned, violence was a thing associated with alcohol, and had no connection to food whatsoever.

In the middle of supper, our most distinguished family guests finally made their appearance. Like almost every other year, they'd flown to Ljubljana, taken a train, first class, to Murska Sobota, and a taxi to Vučja Vas. The aunt and uncle proudly stepped over the threshold. They had Greta between them, leading her by the hands as though she were disabled and would immediately collapse without their support, or disintegrate into dust and then everyone would know that they didn't have a real daughter. She created quite a stir. My relatives got up from the table, shook hands with the English, and patted Greta. "This is our little Greta! She's one of us now!" they exclaimed, and the eyes of some seemed to water with emotion. The women clasped their hands to their breasts and didn't really dare touch her much. And I was consumed with profound envy.

The English child was slender like me, only a bit taller. She had a gentle face, long blonde hair pulled back severely into a ponytail, and unusually piercing eyes. Greta's outfit was simple, a dark blue skirt and a shirt with a bright pattern, similar to mine, except that everything looked nicer on her, better quality, more expensive, yet discreet. Her demeanor differed completely from that of any child I'd met until then; she behaved almost like an adult, perfectly composed and unperturbed, with only her darting gray-green eyes betraying the fact that she felt uncomfortable and disoriented in her role. She shook hands with determination, repeating her "how do you do" in a soft voice with the aplomb of an adult. It was so obvious she came from a different, capitalist country, a country I could never simply visit the way she could mine, by taking a plane, a train, and a taxi. I suddenly realized how impatiently I was waiting to be introduced to her, so that I could touch her. But the English never introduced their adoptive daughter to us children. I could sense that our country relatives' children had their noses put out of joint by all the fuss made over Greta. I would've so much liked to join them in their expressions of resentment—which until then had been directed like a conspiracy against my own city background—since I felt that Greta and I were immeasurably far apart. I no longer clearly knew which side I was on.

After enough approval had been expressed in looks and words by the assembled company, the English aunt quickly reached inside her alligator leather bag. I knew: from that ugly handbag she always produced the sour English candy. This time I wasn't afraid I'd be made to ask and thank her for it in English—I had a pretty strong hunch my relatives wouldn't dedicate any special attention to me this time. I expected the aunt to hand the candy over to Greta for her to distribute among the children, and then we could all go outdoors to play and leave the adults alone. That was the custom. But no; the aunt dealt out the candy herself, albeit somewhat distractedly, failing to notice that some kids got as many as five or six pieces, while others barely got one.

Greta continued to stand bolt upright next to her adoptive father, who stared ahead proudly with a restrained smile, and paid no attention to anyone now that she was through with meeting and greeting people. She didn't so much as look at my candy-distributing aunt, as though these foreign customs were devoid of meaning and none of her concern. No, Greta wasn't our equal. Someone told her to take a seat. She sat down, or rather, climbed onto a tall chair, and softly said thank you. Then out of the blue she turned and looked straight at me, searchingly, as though she weren't altogether certain whether I differed enough from the other children so that I could be a distant cousin of hers. I felt wooden, trapped, as if obliged to say something, of course assertively, yet without being pushy. But I was at a total loss for words. Greta averted her eyes, and everyone seated at the table started posing simple questions to her, about school, England, the weather. She answered in flawless Slovenian, in short, clear sentences. So she knew Slovenian already. I could detect no trace of anything foreign in her accent, except perhaps the unnaturally long pauses that were a giveaway in the longer sentences.

Grandma propelled me toward the table. She gripped me firmly by the elbow and leaned to whisper in my ear that I shouldn't just stand by the wall like a wooden idol and should go talk to my cousin instead. I yanked my arm free and sat down at the table resentfully. Grandma hissed through clenched teeth— the others were naturally not supposed to hear any of this, particularly not the English—that, as usual, I wasn't behaving myself as befitted girls my age and that good manners showed in one's attitude to newcomers—and that was a thing even kids dumber than myself could get into their heads. And I'd never get that English language into my head either if all I was ever going to do was stand on the sidelines in such an incompetent fashion. "She's not my cousin!" I hissed back through equally clenched teeth. "It's not 'she,' but Gretica! What way is that to speak of people!" Grandma furiously shook my elbow. "It's not Gretica, but Greta! And she's not my cousin!" At that Grandma shook me even harder: "Even though she's adopted, it's like she's their real daughter now!" Of course, that was the issue that hung unspoken in the air the entire time. Many of the people had probably wanted to tell the English that they understood completely why they'd adopted a child, but on the other hand everyone was reluctant to be the one to broach such a sensitive subject. "That's not what I meant. The English aren't really my aunt and uncle!"—"That's not for you to decide!" said Grandma almost at the top of her voice and pushed my elbow away, almost tossing it away, like some annoying object.

After dinner we children went out to play on the grass in the backyard, following the orders of the adults. The village children, who of course formed a tightly knit group, played blindman's bluff among them, excluding Greta and me. I sat on the wooden well, on the half covered with planks, and observed Greta from under my scowling eyebrows. The aunt had brought her to the threshold, indicated that she should sit on the steps, and after that Greta never budged. Her duty was to be civil and sit in the company of children, but it didn't include having to play with them. I tried to think of a way to get her involved in some game where I could compete with her, naturally in a way that would give me an advantage. I was still unsure which side I was on, and I have to admit that puzzled me significantly. Despite my doubts, I screwed up my courage and approached her. "What games can you play?" I asked her in the local dialect. I think I was pleased with the audacity of my question, and over-whelmingly excited by the opportunity to observe her from up close. She could barely make out the meaning of my words since she'd only learned standard Slovenian, and I couldn't help but think that she deserved it. "I take ballet lessons," she answered after a longish pause. "What about you?" That caught me slightly by surprise. I wanted to know about games, I didn't care about ballet, piano or flute lessons, the Girl Scouts, chess club and similar extracurricular activities for bored children who had too much of everything sticking out of their asses, as my grandma used to say. "What about me?"

Just then, the father of one of my country cousins came from around the shed. He was carrying an ax, with the sharp end carelessly slung over his shoulder. He stopped by the chopping block, pressed a finger against his left nostril and blew his nose onto the ground, as though he weren't quite certain whether he was beginning or ending the job. After some deliberation, he eased the ax off his shoulder and stuck it in the chopping block with one hand. Just as he was, presumably, about to start gathering wood from the woodpile, his wife showed on the doorstep, grim and fed-up as always, and indicated with two annoyed flaps of her arms that she needed his help right away. He cursed, nodded, and wobbled into the house.

"I can kill chickens, you know," I said out loud. I tried to make it sound as much like a threat as I could. Greta gave me a somewhat cold look, almost reproachful. Probably due to that children and violence thing, which her adoptive parents preached about quite unnecessarily. Just as they used candy to punish ignorance. My claim was of course far from true—I'd never slaughtered a chicken in my life. I'd only been present a few times when my grandma had prepared chickens for slaughter, usually on the occasion of some religious holiday or anniversary. She'd walk about the chicken coop very seriously, and search for the right chickens with an almost transfigured expression on her face, although she'd known for at least a month in advance which chickens were due at the next festivity. But Grandma maintained that the chickens prepared to die by themselves—one had to be able to look them in the eye and read there a certain kind of cloudiness, which appeared as a result of too much suffering in this world. Slaughtering chickens without reading their eyes first was a great sin. She always picked three chickens. She tied their feet together with string near the claws and carried them, one by one, holding them by the string so that their heads hung down, to the butchering lawn by the woodshed. She placed them near the blue-enameled iron bowl into which she caught the blood from their severed necks. Before the actual deed she spat three times into the white interior of the bowl, inhaled deeply, and cautioned me one last time to take three steps back. Just before slaughter the chickens always fell silent; they lay quite still, apparently lifeless, their bound feet now caught in a spasm, while their eyes, upside down, were rhythmically devoured by the pink membrane of their lids. Their beaks, which had squawked loudly only moments before, were now wide open and quivering mutely. I thought they were thirsty.

Greta got to her feet and, ready to go, straightened her skirt. I hadn't expected her to display interest in slaughtering chickens. Possibly she was just going along with the flow, or she might've simply been being polite. There was no time for pondering these questions, though. I quickly stepped up to the chopping block and grabbed hold of the heavy ax. I was fully aware that there was something terribly wrong with this venture, though I could remember all the details about spitting and such. "It's quicker if you use an ax," I said, more to myself than to her. We went to the back of the house where my relatives had built the chicken coop, a shoddy affair of rotten planks hastily nailed together. On the way I picked up a perforated iron pan, which was otherwise used for roasting chestnuts. I also knew which chicken I'd pick: the unevenly mottled gray one, which reminded me of a runty puppy. I leaned over the planks, grabbed the mottled creature by its wing, and pulled it out of the coop. "Look at the eyes." Greta looked at me in surprise. "Not mine, the chicken's!" She looked at the chicken, whose head jerked nervously as it squawked unevenly, and after a while, perhaps thinking she should make some observation, she said: "It doesn't have any teeth."—"No, of course not," I said impatiently. "Now spit into the pan once. But not through the holes." Greta stepped up to the pan and spat out a gob of saliva, then quickly retreated a few steps, as though she knew already that one shouldn't stand too close to the butcher. Now everything was set for the final act, and I began to worry how I was going to calm down the chicken enough to chop off its head. I grabbed it across the wings and set it down on an old tree stump near the coop. I pressed its body downward and, surprisingly, the chicken remained perched there, blinking sleepily into the late afternoon sun. It looked more dead than alive in other respects too—my grandma would've chosen it for slaughter for sure. I derived courage from that thought. The mottled monster began to peck at the wood fungus growing at the edge of the tree stump, thus unwittingly exposing its neck. I quickly put the pan down next to the tree stump and grabbed the heavy ax. I wouldn't get another opportunity as good as this one. I lifted the ax, raising it far back over my shoulders as I'd seen men do when chopping wood, then I swung forward, toward the tree stump. What happened next had little to do with my plans— for, having half closed my eyes with the exertion, I'd slightly missed the chicken's neck. Instead, I chopped its head in two, right across the eyes. I thought the chicken cried out, although its beak bounced off together with the rest of the top part of its head. It might've been Greta who made the sound. Before I could think of something to do with the headless corpse, it had leaped off the tree stump and dashed, or rather fluttered, toward the wood. Even though the wildly flapping wings beat against the undergrowth, the headless freak quickly vanished into the tall grasses. Of blood there was actually fairly little. There was practically none in the pan, only the ax was bloody. I wiped it off on the grass as well as I could, and covered the severed half of the chicken's head with the perforated pan—I figured the maggots and the rain would do their job and my relatives need never find out anything. And besides, they'd surely not miss such an ungainly chicken.

Greta was still standing in the same spot. I was afraid to meet her eyes, but her face looked calm, only a bit inquiring, as though she expected some kind of closure to enable her to make some sense of this game. There was no closure though. All I could think of was that I should've used a knife instead of the ax. I thought I saw Greta give a tiny smile. I still didn't dare look her in the eye—now I was embarrassed. Her cheeks were spattered with a few drops of blood. I don't think she would've minded that, even if she'd known. Again I felt the desire to touch her.

Then we washed in the rainwater that had gathered in a large barrel standing in the middle of the yard. Greta went back and sat on the steps submissively.

"There's no water left in the well, you know," I said. Greta looked at me attentively. Possibly she thought there was some play on words involved. "I believe the well is full," she said deliberately and distinctly. "How can you believe anything, seeing as you've never seen the bottom?"—"I have too," she insisted more softly, no longer certain she could take the game in a prearranged, but to her unfamiliar, direction. "Come! I'll show you!" I took hold of her hand without gentleness and pulled her off the steps. I wondered whether I could beat her at wrestling, and whether it'd make me happy to twist her skinny arm behind her back and force her to make a fist and tremble in rebellion. Who knows if she would've put up a fight. I couldn't assess her strength, though, because she offered no resistance whatsoever, she just gave in without struggle or cooperation, only following me absently. "Now look very closely!" I ordered her and stepped onto the rotting wooden crate leaning against the side of the well. I leaned over the edge of the well and carefully inspected its interior. The evening sunrays illuminated it approximately halfway down the shaft, while on the bottom the contours of boulders could be made out, and the overturned bucket that had lain there ever since the rope broke. Then I straightened up and stepped off the crate: "So there: there's no water in the well. Now it's your turn." I expected her to recoil and hesitate, since children generally didn't dare look over the edge of the well, which we were forbidden to do anyway. But Greta stepped onto the creaking crate without a moment's hesitation and boldly leaned over the edge. I don't know; perhaps she'd never before seen an outdoors well. "Look deep!" I ordered again. When she stood tiptoe on the crate and leaned really far over the edge, I again experienced that unfamiliar excitement, only more intense this time, with my heart beating close to my mouth, since now I was in complete control of the game; I knew Greta was powerless, now really completely dependent on me. I quickly stepped up behind her back and kicked at the crate, sending it flying from under Greta's feet. I heard her cry out in surprise. Not in fear, only surprise. It probably hadn't fully sunk in what had happened. I had the impression she was first slightly jerked over the edge and only then back toward the ground. She gripped the wooden edge firmly, as though falling backward to the ground would be as grave as falling down the well. She probably lost her bearings in the sudden terror and simply gripped the rim lest she fall anywhere. Before her feet landed on the ground I leaped behind her back, grabbed her around the middle and pressed her to me slightly. She still held onto the edge in a paroxysm of fear, as though that was the only way she was going to save herself, and she no longer seemed conscious of my presence. Perhaps she was already experiencing the downward pull. My grandma used to spook us children by telling us that looking into the depth of the well was dangerous because the well could exert such a downward pull that you couldn't and wouldn't want to go away until you forgot completely where and who you were. Greta certainly looked that way already. The thought of Greta having attained a special state unknown to most, and of me being her only remaining link with this world, filled me with unspeakable exhilaration—I closed my eyes to preserve the stolen moment of her enchantment and my absolute supremacy for as long as possible. Then I suddenly panicked for fear that I wouldn't be able to tear her away from the edge and bring her back from her trance. She was heavy in my arms, cumbersome, and her fingers gripping the edge of the well had turned blue like those of a dead person. I shut my eyes even tighter, lest I be drawn into the depths. My palms slid under her shirt and slithered up her sweaty skin. I felt her nipples under the tips of my fingers. I never imagined I'd be touching Greta in this way, I thought, puzzled, during a game I could no longer control or understand. I was afraid her sweaty little body would slip through my fingers and plummet down the dark shaft of the well. I partly opened my hands to get a better grip, but they slipped on her sweaty, thin chest. Her nipples bent unwillingly under my fingers; they were small, but harder and tauter than mine, probably because of her fear. Greta seemed to start breathing only then: her chest filled with air forcefully and her stomach caved in, so that her buttocks pressed hard against my crotch. I was incapable of doing anything anymore, I just grabbed her harder, while my hands nervously slid up her belly, chest, neck. We panted in unison, united by a common terror, in an uncontrollable, unsupportable trancelike state, and I couldn't tell whether my head was spinning or if we were really rocking forward and backward, toward the well and back to the ground . . . It was completely independent of us where the wild rhythm might stop, above the well or on the ground, if it were to stop at all.—Then I felt a hand on my shoulder. I hugged Greta so hard that my eyes welled up. I hoped that whoever it was would understand what was going on, as it would've only taken a single false move for Greta to fall to a place where all games ended. And Greta smelled of milk—not whole milk, not just any milk, but that special UHT milk, which doesn't lose its tantalizing smell so quickly. "No, Greta!" I shouted to the hand on my shoulder. "Please!" Immediately Greta's grip on the edge of the well loosened, she effortlessly straightened up, and my hands fell out from under her shirt, slithering off her body powerless and lifeless. The enchanted embrace had been unlocked. The next instant, a torrent of agitated English burst forth from my aunt's mouth, which, compared to the abyss above which Greta and I had been hanging, now meant nothing at all. From that moment on I no longer cared one way or another about my English relatives, as though I'd suddenly realized their behavior was completely ungrounded and self-serving. Greta, who had of course understood the English outburst, equally didn't seem to take her adoptive mother's words to heart. She looked at me with tired, red-rimmed eyes and smiled. This pushed her mother's anger over the edge. She slapped her, but in such a nervously dignified manner that her palm barely scraped the top of Greta's head, loosening her hair from the already disheveled ponytail. "Your room is on the second floor to the left," my aunt said in Slovenian, obviously so that I too should understand the kind of trouble I'd gotten us both into. That was far from the passionate wrath of my grandma, who would've undoubtedly told me to get myself off to bed that very instant and not let her set her eyes on me again, although it meant exactly the same thing. "And you, young lady," my aunt turned to me, "have behaved most deviously. What's the meaning of that blood behind the house? And the ax? And this dangerous tomfoolery at the well? What's wrong with you?" I expected her to add in her supercilious fashion that she'd have to talk to my grandma about all those things, but she apparently presumed I'd seek out grandma myself, confess everything and ask for appropriate punishment. Fat chance of that; I wouldn't have gone and asked for punishment in any language. "Most deviously," my aunt ended dryly and followed Greta into the house. I touched my forehead and looked at my palm—it was sweaty.

I found my grandma next to the barrel of water in which Greta and I had washed; she was cleaning the blood-covered pans. "There was a lot of blood this year," she said, talking to herself. "It was a good pig. Oh, yes, very good."—"Grandma, when's the right time to kill chickens?" I asked, though I didn't want to think about that chopped off half of chicken head with the crest and the beak and half an eye. "They won't be this good at Christmas. Things change," Grandma went on talking to herself, as though she hadn't heard me. I knew she first needed to finish her conversation with herself. "What do you mean— kill? You don't kill anything, it's a sin to kill. Of course it's a sin. You slaughter chickens." It crossed my mind that there were probably so many sins in the world one was bound to commit at least half of them unwittingly before one got to know them all. And who could say what English sins were. Our relatives never spoke of sins. Grandma straightened up and threw the last of the pans she'd cleaned onto the pile next to the barrel. She wiped the perspiration off her brow with a blood-caked dishcloth and looked at me. The whites of her eyes were full of yellowish specks—I probably noticed them because of the glowing red sunset toward which she was turned. "And never at the same time as you slaughter pigs."—"Is that a sin?" I asked, now calm. "No, that's a curse."—"Is a curse worse than a sin, Grandma?" I was worried. "You don't understand about those things yet. A curse is neither good nor bad in itself. It just is. To marry a chicken and a pig in blood, that's a curse. A curse of the unholy."

I noticed dusk had fallen.

TRANSLATED BY TAMARA SOBAN

BELOW ZERO

November

A few days before the first of November I meant to write your mother a letter. I set aside three full days for it—I didn't leave my apartment, go to the store, the bank, or the post office, and I didn't answer the phone—and I thought that with that sort of determination I'd finish it that much sooner. I almost finished writing it. I've had an envelope bearing the right amount of postage—minus the address, of course—in my lower desk drawer along with all my other important documents for several months now, which is why the stamp dates to Red Cross Solidarity Week. But when it came to signing the letter, something went wrong. As usual, I changed my mind and burned it.

Who really wants to hear some truth about their daughter on the anniversary of her death? And try to understand it? There were so many contingencies. No. When it came time to sign it, my blood ran cold. And I sobered up. And then there's something else. I have the sense that your mother never particularly liked me. Perhaps I only think that on account of some things that you told me. I never had any particular impression of her, but that may be because I never especially looked her straight in the eye. You know me, every morning, whenever I could, I put on my clothes as quickly and quietly as possible and disappeared. Out of your attic room, down the creaky wooden staircase and into the wide, ceilingless day. Each time I locked the door behind me and tossed your keys in the mailbox, I always felt relieved.

Your mother supposedly said that all the other girls were at least your age or younger. And most of all attractive, talkative, and tanned. And women. Perhaps it was tasteless when you woke me up in the morning, tossed me your pajamas, and said I should come down to the kitchen for coffee. I felt like some stupid intruder—staring at the floor like a schoolgirl—you can imagine it's not exactly pleasant to sit at breakfast with ugly bags under your eyes and chapped lips, wearing pajamas that belong to mommy's little girl. That's why I felt guilty. I stared at the teddy bears on your pajamas, at my freezing bare feet, and all of it, including the fact that I felt I didn't dare ask for slippers, reminded me that it was time once again for the litany of eternal traumas that would be pressing me down soon, giving me a chance from close up to look into the cracks between the kitchen floorboards. Who knows, maybe I'm carrying some hidden disease, something—you know—contagious. Not that my complexion was sallow . . . but all those strange thoughts of mine aren't so readily concealed by a suntan. Or spoken. That's why I was afraid that things were building toward another episode that would last several days. I was filled with the same ominously vague thoughts that found no expression in words or the spaces between them—they barely left any faint trace on the tips of my fingers. It's true, I never quite knew after how many cups of coffee to say no, thanks, so as not to add impudence to my bizarreness. I didn't know and—I couldn't have said it, anyway. That's why I didn't try and instead just kept quiet—who knows what all might have rumbled and crashed and seeped out through the bunched up quotation marks, had I opened my mouth.

But you told your mother that beauty isn't everything. If that's what you really said—I don't know what was true after all. If by some chance you're somewhere close by, I don't know, in some formless shape in the air or under the dresser, you're probably wondering what I'm going on about. I know you don't remember all that. None of it, as long as it doesn't have to do directly with you. And you're probably trying to persuade me how fitting and nice it would be if I did send your mother a letter. Because I write such interesting ones, it wouldn't be right if I kept it all pent up. And presumably because she's asked you so many times why I don't come to visit you. As if it was possible to live between some "you" and some "us." Don't you see, I haven't been able to come visit you, because there was no us for me to come from. No, this is my weak spot. So quit hoping. I know how calculating you can be. You know full well how much a single letter like that could cost me. But you just don't change, do you?

And thankfully, I can't hear a thing.

II

It was in January. A dry frost. The snow crunched under our boots as we got into your car. I wondered—I tried to imagine the two of us—what it would be like if it had been above zero. I left my friends and a half-empty bottle on the bar. I simply walked out with you. Without a word to anyone. You drove fast, as though you knew I'd barely just learned your name and might change my mind any instant and tell you to drive me home or, better yet, drop me off at the next corner. You asked if I was afraid. No, there was no fear. As long as everything passed as quickly as possible and it was morning again and I was already at the nearest bus stop, hunched over in the bitter predawn cold, stamping my feet and wondering which way—right or left— would take me to town.

That's how it began. Entirely by accident. And anything else would be an invention. Only now do I admit that I was driven by curiosity. Because I'd never yet slept with an active and I wanted to know what it was like when a woman doesn't allow you to touch her. What it means to be an object for another woman, what the power game is like when biology isn't fate. Or something like that. I don't know—as if it mattered anymore. I certainly wasn't allowed to connect to any meaning, so I've no idea what good anatomy would've done me.

Yes, I liked you. Through all of it I still liked you. Over morning coffee—you caught me as I was hurriedly buttoning up my jacket and trying to dig a bus token out my tight jeans pockets—you lured me back into your fantasies. Put on your pajamas. The male ones with the vertical stripes. Even though I didn't want to get too much into your skin. Do you realize I didn't even know what color your nipples were, or how your skin creased when you lay on top of me.

It's true—I dreamed about you a few days before the first of November. It was probably the dream that led me to the ill-considered act of composing a letter to your mother. It was a strangely calm dream. You and I, alone, inside a bright, spacious room. I remember the big windows and some square, silver pipes. You lay naked on the biggest pipe and I was leaning over you. I held my hands, sticky from white dough, up in the air with the index and little fingers extended. You were so salty.

I don't know why that dream, of all things. In fact there was only one time when I managed to sneak up on your crotch. When I tasted you, you went blue in the face—that's the impression I had. You squeezed my neck. I could feel that you both wanted and hated it. Then you grabbed me by the hair and pulled my head up toward you. I didn't know what you wanted. Then, with the back of your free hand, you slapped me in the face. I noticed my response, a sweet spasm in my crotch. I didn't know what you wanted. You hit me in the face, and then I felt warm, and blood as viscous and salty as your juices dampened my mouth, which had gone dry from fast breathing, and I'd like to know if you felt as crazy as I did. Or if you were just that hateful, that furious. Perhaps because you'd warned me not to get mixed up with you. Or did you just feel that crazy. I'd like to know. Or was it because I'd told you, out of nowhere, apparently, that nobody gets away from me. I don't know why, what came over me, I didn't mean anything by it.

And there was no carefully fashioned blindfold at all, like the ones they write about, just an ordinary cotton kerchief, because I had a sore throat that day.

I also considered writing your mother about that.

III

Very soon I found out that I wasn't good at obeying you. You'd provoke me, sometimes implore me, who knows what all you tried, but it was impossible to respond in kind. Much less do your bidding. Fine, you made it look like I was the only one who couldn't get close, as though I was just too different, too radically different for you to be able to commit yourself to. At least not in this world. But I was a refuge of everything different, life hadn't beaten me, loneliness didn't exist for me. After my days-long episodes were over I felt much better—then I could express myself, but I had to begin with questions written all over the place, in the time and space of folds of skin. And if anything had ever been even the tiniest, most approximate bit all right, I wouldn't have had to make such beastly efforts. I never knew what you wanted. Once you asked me where I got all those questions from that seemed so sudden and unexpected to you. From your answers; I had no idea what else to tell you. And because each and every one of those answers slapped me so heedlessly—and I was afraid of new ones—I sometimes wanted to know how the story would end. Maybe that's why I finally forced it, determined it myself.

And when you told me that you didn't like me in jeans and with my hair slicked down under my cap, it came to me in a flash that an end had to be put to this. Because I came across tough that way? Come on, I could never have had long, blonde hair so you could fall in love with me, as though I still wanted to waste time trying to obey you better, let alone mess with anatomy.

Gradually I began to lower you below zero. I wanted to tell

you, signal to you, but how was I supposed to do that? You never heard what I said, and I never had anything of yours, nothing to bind you to and protect you from me. And everything I gave you cheated me, eluding my grasp, without even the phantom travails of severed umbilical cords. And if you took too long to slide down my body, I'd contract, grow impatient, my head would nod down to my knees and my stumps would slough off, little symbols shooting past my eyelids, and I became pleasantly strange and unfamiliarly beautiful, as though undergoing metamorphosis when I closed my eyes in delight. And how many times did I have to hold back from sinking my claws in your temples and shoving your head down, somewhere far below, at last beyond, beneath the line where everything turns to ice. Including fury. Let alone words or reasons.

The last night I spent with you, you'd already passed into the next decade. That's why it's easier for me today. Of course I know that you intended to live long, but I unexpectedly, brutally kept that from happening. I know everything. But it's easier for me—for *me*—because you'd already taken on that burden.

I called to tell you to come to Ljubljana as we'd already agreed, but you tried so inconsiderately and clumsily to wriggle out of it. In fact you simply ignored me. I've always hated that, don't you realize. When somebody brought me to the point where I had to beg. But you explained how warm it was there, and that the sun was shining—in between instructions you were giving to somebody in the background what to take along for a picnic—some people were even going into the water and you would've, too, if you weren't already so pleasantly high. Oh yes, and there are lots of people at our place, they've driven out from Ljubljana where it's always so boring on weekends. As though you didn't know that I didn't have any "our place," which wasn't just seen as abnormal, it was diseased, but you had to take your pokes at me and stir up my traumas, as though malicious irritability were more real than the danger of my fugitive thoughts.

Oh, of course you'll come, you just don't know when—*how to create a different kind of world.* You've always overlooked that. There are so many people around you and you're completely distracted, or whatever. This whole shower of meaningless words that are left hanging like patches of porous skin on the never-changing framework of imaginary states. You can imagine—because you know me so well already, not because you sensed anything during that conversation—how I was clenching my teeth and my muscles and sweating into the receiver. Once, I'd wanted to take away from you what you referred to as so many people. Actually, take you away from them, just pluck your head out of the sand, but somebody ought to tell them . . . because then maybe there could be a completely different kind of summertime without any sun, and then lots of people would flock to ski slopes and you'd be dialing my number again to yank some other strap on my straitjacket—I'll bet they're still sending you postcards and greetings and contorting their faces and writing with idiotic red felt pens, as if to say "guess who sends you hugs, hugs, hugs," as though they had no idea you weren't reading them anymore. And that you'd have no idea who all the hugs, hugs, hugs were from. But why bother, your mother enjoys them and you—if you're still here in the air somewhere or under the dresser—think it's nice that you knew how to take up so much space that some people still insist on addressing cards to you—regardless of whether you exist or not. Yes, all those connections. But I had to work so hard for that. I'm your last connection. To life.

What a fucking zombie.

Even before my speechless thoughts had run out you'd hung up the phone. Maybe you even forgot to tack on that you loved me. I could be very grateful to you for that lack of manners.

But some other time.

IV

A few less slips.

Now I'm convinced that your call was decisive, or maybe that you dialed my number only because you already knew it by heart. Although that probably wasn't the first time. I don't know why precisely that phone call. Why everything couldn't end this time, too, with another episode lasting several days, followed once again by the suppression of all the same endless, lurking, boringly bitter stuff somewhere below zero.

At least this time I didn't get caught on some bend of the spiral and was able to back up a bit, toward the top. It was dark, unbearably dark. Translucently gloomy, in fact, when you still stand a chance of glimpsing something. Sort of like I was suddenly on some German autobahn on a cold winter night, far from all exits, as though all of the gas stations had vanished. And I strain my eyes, because I know I should be able to see something—even though the spiral has no bottom.

You were at home. One of those days when the words didn't come to you so easily. But I could hear so very much. I was thirsty. But I didn't say for water. Something told me—at least this time—that before I got there you'd had a visitor and you were unhappy with something. But that happened a lot. You'd also fall silent each time you so innocently and quietly wished I'd go. Disappear.

This evening, however, your silence began when you opened the door. Your ill disposition upset and confused me, and I felt incensed by the insidious feeling of your eyes maliciously flashing each time I turned away. Aimed at the nape of my neck. But that made it easier. I felt better with my back shot through than under the usual heap of nice words.

If you hadn't begun to undress without even looking at me—just didn't feel like it, huh?—I might yet have gone. But I didn't budge—what difference did it make with your eyes closed? You climbed in naked under the sheets and waited—for what?—for me to come join you or start talking, bugging you and making demands—it didn't matter which to you. You drew on your cigarette and the corners of your mouth twitched—but why—and of course you hoped I'd eventually go. That it'd be easier for me to leave "with something." But how empty that something always became as soon as I let go of the handle on the other side of the door . . . I was amazed at how I could look at you, realizing that I looked at you the same way I used to spend hours staring transfixed at stars about which I'd read in the introduction to some atlas that they'd gone extinct ages ago. And only the hopeless distance between us and them made it still possible for us to see them. The news hadn't yet reached us that they were no more. Such coincidences, such shameless mercies—those cosmic distances. Like a firm connection in a time when worlds, when surfaces are flying apart.

I said fine, all right—you said nothing—all right then, but that I wanted to really make love. Because that evening, at least, there were no terrors and my eyes weren't being drawn into the cracks. Why does that even happen to me?

When I undressed, I asked you to turn your back to me. So that I wouldn't be looking at something I'd never seen. You sat up in bed and put your cigarette out—*how can you not look at me*. As though I'd had my moments of bliss. Still wearing my jeans when I sat down on the bed behind your back. I was on the verge of telling you that everything, whatever that may be, but in any case everything would soon be over, that in spite of the mounting passion and pulsation of my body this wouldn't take much effort. And that afterwards I'd go without saying a word, without a reproach, without disappointment. With no secret longing to come back—*to life*.

This'll be it, this time I'm through.

I still had the cotton kerchief clenched in my teeth. It was unbearably hot. I glanced down at my breasts. Drops of sweat were falling from my hard nipples onto my jeans and the sheets. I could hear them. My jaw unclenched, we came disconnected and you dropped face down onto the sheets. At that very instant it flashed through my head that that phrase—you dropped face down—had been so deeply drilled into me by movies, novels, and dreams that it ultimately had to drag me down after it, way down below the line, and it was only fitting for me to eject it—along with you. Along with you.

Yes, the blindfold had slipped from my eyes onto my nose, then down over my mouth, and from there down to my neck— at least I think so, though I can't recall exactly. And me, I had my eyes closed, since I can't look when I'm coming . . . And then came your moans. I still had my eyes shut—shut tight, not even a sliver of light got through as you came, it was all too real for either of us to have faked it, I had no real awareness what all was around me. How much of me or anyone else was there. Anatomy had been wiped out.

I dried myself with your T-shirt and tossed it into the corner. You lay there, your back possibly still glistening with sweat. I didn't bend down to see better. I knew I was never going to touch you again. A few days later . . . even I don't like you that unattractive and bluish . . . thank goodness, I almost began to be bitter.

I got dressed and dug the token out of my pocket. I spent nearly a half hour shivering at the bus stop, it was very cold with damp fog and I imagined there were little lights flickering on tiny Christmas tree on the other side of the shuttered windows.

For several weeks I was nowhere to be found—that's what the people who know me and don't bother to look me up would've said. I never did buy all those newspapers. I couldn't be bothered with that. You know, I left you lying face down and I hoped that your eyes were shut. That you didn't spend the whole week that followed with your eyeballs scraping the sheets—that would've made me imagine you staring at me forever, accusing me of some equally disagreeable thing. I swear I had thoughts like that for several months afterwards. On account of that blackened mirror you loaned me once when my eyes were all red. Then you made up that you'd given it to me.

There've been so many times when I've wanted to tell someone about all these coincidences, these messages wrapped up in distances, these uncoordinated encounters in time. All these blank contexts—they're left over from some sort of "us." Fortunately nobody ever came to ask me about them. Sometimes I imagined that during the whole week that went by before you were found your hair and nails grew out quite a bit. Your eyelashes, too, and your eyebrows, or maybe the hairs in your nostrils. Then they'd have to realize: there's nothing to find here, nothing to ascertain. It's too late to make any judgments, you'd been given your cross long ago. And you behaved so well.

But nobody ever came. Not even you. I often look at that little mirror, sometimes it's as though I were looking at your back, so I turn it around, shake it, and stroke its black spots with my fingers . . . Still. Maybe the cats knead because they see themselves in the mirror? We used to assume that they didn't.

December

I packed my things and moved a few weeks ago—admittedly, as far from your room as possible—and untied my shoes, because it goes faster with claws. Because I didn't go back after that business with you, and I remain disconnected. That's why I haven't had any more episodes or restlessness in my life. The spiral swallows you up. Only one thing has surprised me: I have more dimensions now, more features, even more arms and legs—almost as though I had no body at all.

TRANSLATED BY MICHAEL BIGGINS

SEWING THE PRINCESS

Finally the day had come. I got up, went into the bathroom, brushed my teeth, washed my hands, even though they didn't get dirty from sleeping, and got dressed. I sat down at the kitchen table and for the first time in a long while waited submissively and without complaint for my much-hated breakfast. This day I even consented to fried bread, even though it had been ages since I'd found every conceivable variation on fried eggs revolting. I even managed to drink my coffee with milk without making a face—it always tasted several days old, despite being freshly brewed. None of it mattered—I still preferred having my mandatory, awful breakfast with mother and grandma to going on some agonizing school field trip to see old castles that had been nothing more than boring, overgrown ruins for centuries, so that you got precious little history out of them, mainly just a bitter taste from all the vomiting on the bus. Lately I'd been throwing up a lot more, including during gym class, which meant that "for the time being," as it said in a note from the school to my parents, I didn't have to do phys ed. Or go on school field trips. The only time I was still forced to socialize was during class. Actually not even during class, where you could listen to the teacher for a change and ignore all your classmates yakking. The only time I had to socialize—or rather, try to avoid socializing—was during recess. Dawdling in the toilet stall next to a stinking toilet was a very handy option, until they started to bang on the door and threaten to drag off any loiterers who were hogging the toilets not to smoke or to poop, but for no good reason at all. In spring it was easier. In spring I could go out to the schoolyard and hang out under the trees on the other side of the street, where we really weren't supposed to go, but our class monitor made an exception in my case and I was allowed to cross the street. (Though she was careful to add that I was doing it at my own risk.) In short, that I had a right to relieve myself in private. That was the only way I could get any peace.

Take care to sew from right to left

Instead of going on a field trip with all the cultureless louts from school I go with mother to see Ilonka the seamstress. This is my day! The best day of the entire school year. Ilonka lives on the other side of town in an old building that stands on a corner, with the result that she lives in two places and you can get to her place down two different streets that are perpendicular to each other, and you can see into her building through two rows of windows. We always go there from the right, as Mother and Grandma say. Taking the shady street that runs alongside a municipal park where kids tend to gather especially around the playground, but then in the early evening hours also the kind of kids who enjoy putting their tripping and name-calling skills to the test. The one good day. Although mother and I approach from the right, we have to go around the corner, because the outside door is on the other side of the building. I ring the bell. I know it'll take a while for the steady rumble of the sewing machine to stop, before we hear the drawn-out "Com-ing!" and then the shuffle that's always reminded me of a gentle zigzag stitch, since the seamstress has one leg shorter than the other and this makes her gait a continuous evasive maneuver. As she unlocks and begins to tug at the door, which has always been too tight in its frame, the pinkish red lettering on an otherwise unobtrusive pale-green wooden sign over the door jiggles slightly. *Ilona Tsch, Schneiderei.* Ilona was Ilonka's mother, but she died long ago and in all that time her daughter has never changed the sign, since there's only one letter's difference between them.

Ilonka always hugged me, holding me tight to her skinny body and the gray-green cardigan sweater that always smelled nicely of threads and tailor's chalk and scissored material. Grandma said that she always hugged me that tight because she was never able to have any children of her own. I suppose because she had one leg shorter than the other. Who would've imagined that the length of your legs could have that kind of effect. Then Ilonka would always shudder, step back while still holding my arms, and muss my hair, saying, "I'd better be careful not to poke you!" Her sweater was always bristling with pins that had shiny metallic or colored heads, needles for sewing by hand or machine, and other tiny metal objects whose purpose is known only to seamstresses and tailors. Then she put one arm around my shoulders and because of her gait, which made her lean to one side, together we made our way at a slight zigzag into the house. It was always with joy that she'd lead me into her huge sewing workshop, which was located right in the corner of the building, so that it took in light from both sides, through all four huge windows.

"The most important thing is the light, but I've told you that already, haven't I?" Again she impishly mussed up my hair. Ilonka the seamstress was the only person who'd completely forget about the adults, in order to spend time with me—and on occasions like going for a visit adults were always incredibly loud and unreasonable and insistent that everyone pay attention only to them.

"So you really want to be a seamstress?" Ilonka asked me. I nodded and blushed. I turned to mother, who opened a big handbag and gave me a big package of material, without feeling the need to say where she'd bought it and how much she'd paid for it. I take the package and ceremoniously set it down on the big sewing table where there's always some patch of free space for new stacks of material or clothing that her customers bring. I look at Ilonka. "Go on, show me!" she says encouragingly.

I rip the paper and unwrap the package, revealing a sumptuous white fabric sewn with shiny embossed roses that merge the colors reflected in them like dim mirrors. Ilonka clasps a hand to her mouth in surprise. And admiration, it seems.

"Tell me what you want me to make of such beauty!" she says without taking her eyes off the material. "This is . . . this is . . . extremely high quality."

I look at mother and smile shyly. Then I say, "A princess."

Ilonka quietly cheers with approval and covers her mouth with both hands. Then at last she sits down, since it's not easy for her to stand, which is something we've known for a long time. Just as we also know that once in her life, but truly just once, she'd wanted to marry and have a family. Her husband-to-be took her with him to Australia, where he'd been working for a number of years. But Ilonka just sat in that Australian apartment and sewed and sewed without being able to speak to a soul. She couldn't understand anything, so she chose not to leave the apartment so that the neighbors wouldn't try to speak to her in English. And when she saw her first kangaroo, she covered her eyes in horror and felt sick. That's what my grandma said. Ilonka packed her things and went to catch the first airplane back to Yugoslavia. Her former fiancé didn't even take her to the airport. "So what are you going to do with this princess's dress?" my mother asked skeptically, as if to imply that you couldn't waste this much money on a Mardi Gras costume.

"For wearing at home," I said.

After school on each of the days that followed I went to sew. At this point I almost forgot about school. I stopped fretting about what might happen to me in the school corridors or out on the playground. Ever since I stopped going straight home from school, turning in the opposite direction, instead, toward the hospital, they let me go in peace. Probably on the assumption that I was still going to get bandaged. Nobody knows that I'm actually going to the seamstress. The doctor had last seen me a few days before. I was coming along fine, he said, though I was more interested in how much longer it was going to take. "Another week or so," he said, which is what he always said. Then he took a good look at my face from close up, touched one of my eyebrows, and said to the nurse, "I don't think we're going to remove these today."

Then he looked me in the eyes again, as though he'd suddenly remembered that this was about me, and assured me with somewhat too big a smile, "It's healing well. They've done a great job. Before long all of that's going to be closed up again, the stitches will have done their job, and at that point we'll give you some ointment to put on the scars. You'll be as good as new by your wedding day!"

I wonder if they also told Ilonka the seamstress, who has one leg too short, that her leg would grow out by her wedding day.

Every time I leave the doctor's office I feel like a hero. Sort of historical, like those ruins that everybody goes to look at must feel. But only until I go through the electric door outside and see the park in front of me. The municipal park with the playground and the menacing thick bushes and the fat tree trunks that conceal rotten hollows inside them. And the brats that call you names and trip you. How convenient that Ilonka's place is so close. And that sometimes, after we've sewn for a long time and it gets dark outside, she sees me home without making any fuss about it at all. And then quietly waddles back through town.

A reverse stitch, used mostly for sewing in zippers, is almost invisible on the surface of the fabric

Grandma says that a Mardi Gras with no snow is no Mardi Gras at all. Even if snow falls after Mardi Gras, it just brings bad luck. And there'll probably be lots of flooding in May. In some mysterious, almost conspiratorial way all of grandma's winter months are bound up with the summer ones. Late snow in March, floods in May. Sausage-making in December means a jagged sun in February, causing everything to rot. A jagged sun is the kind of pale sun that doesn't give any warmth. I have the strong impression that that's just the kind of sun that's been shining this winter. It was unusually bright for a late winter afternoon. In that park where the boys trip people and beat them up. It was the same three boys, the same voices and the same nervous gestures with their heads. Sometimes they'd come to the schoolyard. They noticed me that time when we had gym class outdoors and we had to run and jump half naked. "Hey, look at that bitch," one of them squealed and pointed at me. "Huh? What sort of bitch is that, anyway?" one of the others added. Of course then the third one piled on, the one with long hair, "But at least she's got long legs." That one liked looking at me and his eyes would glint, and so he got most on my nerves. All three of them liked to come to the schoolyard, show off and make fun of those of us who still went to grade school. The long-haired boy's voice always seemed slippery to me, dirty, like the voice of a person who cheers while others do the kicking. He was the one who grabbed me by the neck in the park. With his shaking, sweaty hand. He was the first one who touched me. As his fingers, yellowed from nicotine, slid under my T-shirt, the middle one, whose name was Jailbird, gave me a swift, powerful kick that knocked both of my legs out from under me. He was the town champion in karate while he was still going to school. His picture had once been in the school newspaper. After that it was easy. When you lose your balance, your eyes aren't at the level of theirs anymore.

If you have to stop in the middle of a stitch, be sure to always leave the needle in the fabric.

We've gone all January without any snow, they're saying on our street. Wherever you go, you hear that winter isn't what it used to be, and that there won't be any precipitation in February, either. Which is supposed to be particularly awful, almost like a scaled-down version of the end of the world. The princess's dress is already hanging on one of the dressmaker's mannequins in Ilonka's workroom.

Before Ilonka and I set to work, we always make a little space on the big sewing table where we put our cups and drink our tea in regular, hurried sips, in order to take in the last of the late afternoon light as we admire the white radiance of the half-assembled dress. As we, grimacing, at last take our final sips of the overly hot tea, we still have to turn on the light. One of those big, powerful lights that, in our little town, you otherwise only come across in photographers' studios. Ilonka aims it straight at the dress on the mannequin. First we smooth down all those hanging, uneven pieces of white cloth that are only attached with pins.

The edges of the skin tissue around the wound must be as even as possible, retain good circulation and show no signs of morbidity. The edges and walls must connect along their entire length and depth.

We must leave nothing to chance and shaky, uneven stitches, and we can't even correct any mistakes, because fabric like this doesn't take well to being pierced too many times, Ilonka says. That's why we have to prepare everything on the sewing mannequin beforehand. Sometimes we turn the mannequin, other times we move the light so we can examine the swatches and edges in detail before we sew them together. It's because of these marvelous embossed roses that we have to be especially careful how we assemble the different swatches of fabric. Besides which, under every angle of light the roses shine in a different color and dazzle the eyes, because they reflect everything that's in their vicinity.

Although everything happened so fast that it was impossible to describe it all afterwards in very much detail without having to doubt the veracity of your words, and though my position under the weight of the blows, shoves, and kicks changed very quickly, I do remember the rays of the red evening sun that flooded the patches of snow on the ground in the park. And their eyes—I remember them best of all. The dark eyes of the third one, the oldest, a lifelong outcast from all the schools he'd attended, showed pleasure, a kind of mischievous hope that he was going to experience something so new and extraordinary that it would truly be a shame to miss it. His eyes kept darting in excitement from his friends to my body, and his blows were so imprecise, as though he'd forgotten that you aim with your eyes, not your clenched fists. But I suspect it was precisely his clumsy, slapdash punch that, while it spared my left eyebrow, did serious damage to my eardrum. To this day my schoolmates think my hearing is bad from the attack in the park. In fact, I hear perfectly well now, though I haven't let anyone at school know that.

Jailbird, the former karate black belt, had the kind of chiseled, stocky face that eyes get lost in. In all the photographs in the school paper and on the hallway walls he was eyeless. But when, in the park, he kicked me from behind to get me off balance, his eyes were just as focused as all of his movements. The small pupils amid the blue-gray, tiny and motionless, estimating the distance and in a flash calibrating the force of the punch needed to bridge a particular distance to the goal. As I dropped to the ground the one with long hair still held me tightly by the neck, causing my head to rub against the crotch of his tight jeans. In that fleeting instant all three of them released a sharp, short burst of laughter. Or maybe that wasn't them laughing at all, but laughter from the playground close by. Perhaps that was the park itself laughing, which had at its entrance a sign bearing a message painstakingly inscribed by some third-grade class: *This park is the heart of your community. Take care how you walk through it.*

The boy with long hair had distinct, flashing eyes, actually I recall his quite well, they'd been etched into my memory ever since grade school, and besides tripping the younger girls, he'd feel me up during recess. They were the revoltingly nice eyes of someone who likes to prey on others and were almost always accompanied by a clumsy smacking of his lips, which he must have acquired from watching his older, equally stupid brothers. At one time he still chased me through the park. His pals had long since given up chasing me in favor of far better amusements, but he kept on changing directions, just like me, taking new shortcuts and waiting new places in ambush, which made it hard to avoid him, even with a bicycle. He was always the last to let up. During my extended fall to the ground, as my head slid over the taut denim concealing his crotch, his expression was exactly the same as I remembered it from the school cafeteria—greedy and impatient, for instance as his long arms reached over the heads of the smaller kids to grab the slices of bread that had the thickest layers of spread on them.

"Let it go," Jailbird said just then with the serious voice of a coach who no longer has to shout to be heard and obeyed. When long hair let go of my neck, albeit with one final shove, I worried that my head might collide with the ground unprotected. But then, just at that moment, Jailbird's foot in its winter hiking boot rose toward my face, and I was briefly buoyed by an irrational wave of relief that this boot was going to save me from falling onto the path, which was strewn with sharp, minute gravel that glinted in a thin covering of ice. Once I landed, after having been briefly jerked up in the air by the counterforce of that foot, the gravel turned red and gave the impression of some soft embossing or velvet.

At the corners take care to leave the needle exactly in the corner,
flip up the foot pedal, and turn the fabric around the needle.
Then lower the foot pedal and continue sewing.

We sewed for three weeks, maybe four. As far as I was concerned it could've gone on for a year or more. When we first tried the dress on, we treated ourselves to a glass of champagne that Ilonka had kept stored in her old sideboard for years. It had been meant for her wedding in Australia. I was freezing in just my undershorts and shirt as she carefully took the finished dress off the mannequin, and all that shivering and rattling of my teeth was far from pleasant. The touch of the fabric against my bare skin sent a tingling sensation all down my spine. A bunched petticoat made of coarser starched fabric that Ilonka called an *unterslip* rustled around my thighs like the waters of a babbling brook. When with some finality she pulled a hidden zipper on the left side shut, the dress all at once relaxed around me, and I could feel a tautness in my belly, while my shoulders, which nobody at home or at school had been able to force out of their slump, suddenly straightened up. The lace Cossack collar forced my chin forward and my lower jaw relaxed for the first time since the stitches had been removed. My arms hung relaxed but ready at my sides, as though they knew what they wanted. They were waiting. I still had my eyes closed. I could hear the squeak of the big mirror that Ilonka had turned around so I could see.

"Now open your eyes, princess," she said softly.

After I fell to the ground there appeared to be no life left in me. The final kicks were delivered—abruptly, in quick succession, because everything had gone on too long for a quick payback, and because it was still light outside. I remember a bird that was flying low through the trees and the flapping of its wings. I could still hear their pulse after the bird had flown off. At times it even flapped its wings more loudly, right next to my ears. When one powerful flap of its wing forced my head toward the light ebbing through the tree branches, I saw through my swollen eyelids that the pulsation came from the monotonous, repeated swinging and collision of a foot with my back and head. Long hair was last again. He kept kicking, even though his two friends had clearly already moved on and were probably trying to think of a fitting way to continue an evening that was off to such an exciting start. His snarled hair had gotten caught in the damp, whitish corners of his mouth, out of which there seemed to be coming some distant, irregular sound. When long hair suddenly left my field of vision, a couple of high, black women's shoes entered it, one of which had a much thicker sole. While my brain kept trying to figure out whether the shoe with the thicker sole causing it to make an irregular clunk was the right or the left shoe, giving me an unbearable headache, Ilonka's face bent down over me. Then, still crouching, she straightened her back up and began waving her arms wildly and opening her mouth. Since no sound came out of it, it struck me that maybe the whole time I'd been on the ground I hadn't been able to hear anything, and that the distorted series of sounds was the result of my even more mistaken conclusions about the imaginary sounds and their sources.

Good suturing requires that we select the right type of suture, that the sutures be evenly spaced, extend to just the right depth and connect matching layers of dermis.

Finally I swallow my excitement and take a look in the mirror. The first thing I see is the reflection of my eyes, only not in the mirror's image of my face, but from the raised roses on the dress. Collectively, the perfectly aligned roses reflect everything: my eyes, the zigzag scar on my face, the petite bracelets on Ilonka's wrists under the hands that she holds clasped together in admiration, even her shoes and her hair. My face is radiant. This perfect princess in the mirror is me. I put my hands over my mouth, then my eyes, then my forehead. My excitement is so great I don't know what to do. Ilonka claps her hands, picks up the champagne bottle from the table, shakes it, and forces the cork out with her thumbs. Its pop returns us to reality. We shriek and rush to place our glasses under its gushing foam. The bubbles pleasantly effervesce through our heads. Glasses in hand, we stand at her huge windows, the two on the side of the building that faces the municipal park, the heart of the city, my dress shining in the steel colors of the gray and still young winter night. Ilonka empties her glass and says that anything can be done if it's looked at properly. All dresses are sewn by eye. I'm unable to say a single word.

Make a knot and pull it just tight enough that the edges of the wound touch each other and rise above the level of the surrounding skin.

My parents wanted to move. A change of environment was needed, that's what the school counselors said. Patch up the situation as quickly as possible, to minimize any negative effects on my performance at school. Or on the school's reputation. I don't know if my parents wanted to move at all. I certainly didn't. Moving is actually what the social worker, the counselors, and some of the police wanted us to do. Nicest of all was the detective. Maybe because he had a thousand questions. Because he behaved as though this was our shared concern. That I had to use every moment when my head didn't ache and try to remember their faces. Because they say if you can remember one, the others will follow shortly after that. The last time he visited us was that evening when, a few hours earlier, I'd put on the princess dress at Ilonka's for the first time and the embossed fabric softened my skin. The detective waited patiently for me to come home. He was wondering if I'd remembered anything else. No, nothing at all. I don't know if my attackers said anything, because my hearing is still very bad. I don't remember anything from after I got kicked in the head. Yes, there were three boys, I think. There were probably three boys. No, I don't know their faces or what school they were from. Then, as always, he patted me on the hand and asked me a few boring questions about school and the score of yesterday's soccer game. There isn't much to say about those kinds of things, either. Had perhaps anyone at school ever said anything nasty to me? Nothing in particular, I said. Had anyone ever called me bad names? I suppose, I conceded, sometimes I've been called a bitch, sometimes a heifer. I don't know if those count as bad names. Well, they're certainly not nice ones. Had anyone pushed me? I don't really know, probably everyone. Usually when we play basketball or handball on the school playground, when I can't tell who's doing the pushing. For sure kids were also telling me to get out of their way—in the school hallways, the restrooms, the classrooms, even outdoors. The detective nodded and acted as though he understood. He sipped his coffee, lit a cigarette and got up. When I let escape a sigh of relief, he suddenly raises a finger, as though to say with his mouth full of coffee he can't speak as fast as he's thinking.

"Has anybody ever . . ." He swallows his coffee. "Has anyone ever called you a queer?"

I stare blankly ahead. All of my thoughts are focused on the white dress. The way it captures the light when I raise my arms, the sleeves made elegant by the padding at the shoulders and the extensions sewn from heavier fabric that hang down and give the dress its real character.

The border stitch is barely perceptible and used mainly for sewing in linings. It is also used for fixing a stitch from the surface when it is inaccessible from the underside.

I had to wait until Mardi Gras was over. So they wouldn't know if it was already over or not. So all they would know was that it had been. I pick out a good spot in the bushes. If I stand in the snow by the bushes, my dress and matching shawl made of the same fabric reflect only white and greenish shades.

I become invisible, more or less.

They approach. They have bottles in hand and they're casually chatting. Jailbird, long hair, and the oldest one. They stagger a bit, and then they suddenly stop. All of them look for something in their pockets. Jailbird finds his cigarettes first and offers them to the others. This stop of theirs gives me the perfect opportunity to pick the right light at the right instant. The lit cigarettes slowly come closer. Judging from their voices they're quite drunk, a lot more than they were the last time we met in the park. When the sun drops a little lower, so that it shines at a right angle into the snow at the edge of the path, I come out of the bushes and onto the path to face them. Not all of them see me at the same time. Jailbird is first, and he starts to turn away, thinking that this can't be true, what he's seeing, that he must not be seeing things right. But his twenty-twenty vision has never deceived him before. The raised roses on my princess dress reflect the light of the blazing sun and the reddish snow simultaneously. They look like streaks of blood on the snowy white dress. I just stand there. I thought long hair would be the one to squeal most, but he's actually the first to come to his senses enough to be able to run away, though in his drunkenness he trips over one of the stone pediments that will support a bench in the spring. The oldest one, who has a hard time concealing any excitement, howls and calls his mommy for help, blubbering as he runs away as fast as his legs will carry him, looking back now and then in the rotten hope that the bloody princess will overtake the other two first. Jailbird, swearing, is the only one to think for a moment about maybe taking the ghost on. He's the one who shows the most unalloyed fear, despite the fist he holds up in the air. He's so afraid that he's afraid to run. Then long hair suddenly picks himself up out of the snow. When he looks in my direction, I can see blood on his forehead. Hysterically he waves an arm at Jailbird to get moving, already. Then to save himself, at least, if he can't save his friend, he continues to run helter-skelter and, unable to choose a direction or find a path, he wades with great difficulty through the deep snow. Jailbird charges into the deep snow just as thoughtlessly and follows him as fast as he can.

I just stand amid the floodlit snow and watch as they run away from the reflection of their own eyes in the brilliant roses on the princess dress.

Later, inside, when outside it's already dark and the curtains have been drawn over both rows of windows, Ilonka brings me some tea and wipes the powder off my face with some cotton. She's made me tell her our story about the bloody princess and the three boys twice already, and still she keeps shaking her head and laughing to herself.

"Which one did you say ran the hardest?"

"Your nephew, of course. Even though he's the oldest, he's as quick as lightning."

"I knew it!" she says for at least the fifth time and laughs so hard that she has to gasp for air. "My sister was such a bitchy, mean married woman and mother. Her only virtue was that because her legs were the same length, she didn't think it was important to learn how to sew."

For years now Ilonka has regularly called her *ugly sister*, just as she'd solemnly promised her late mother she would do. For the last few weeks she's been able to endure all her sister's boasting about her house, her cars, and her extremely talented son who's been doing quite well at school, though he's had less luck in other respects. She never forgets to say where-all her son has been, what he's been doing, and especially what he's going to do the next day and the day after that. Ilonka can't help remembering everything about where her nephew is going to go. But now we can relax for a few months. Maybe wait for spring, when the embossed roses will flash in a different sort of way.

"There's been a lot of snow, an unusual amount for this time of year," Ilonka says, using her short leg to drive the old sewing machine.

"There'll be floods in May for sure," I say.

Ilonka stops the sewing machine for a moment, looks out the window, then at me. "Smart boy," she says. Then she smiles.

It's very important to choose the right thread for a stitch, to select the right place for it, to make a secure knot and pull it tight with just the right amount of force.

TRANSLATED BY MICHAEL BIGGINS

A KEY TO THE RESTROOM

On the way back to the city we make a stop at a roadside inn. "We stopped here on the way to visit your mother for the first time," you say. "I like it here. I don't know why, but I do." I nod absentmindedly, wondering whether the apples you and my mother put in the trunk might be bruised from the ride.

We order our usual coffee with milk and drink it with half a packet of sugar and a glass of sparkling water. Waiting impatiently for the waitress to bring us a pack of Gauloises Bleu, I look around the lounge without really seeing anything. Then it strikes me that it's filled almost exclusively with men. The entrances to the restrooms are visible to all. You're exposed when you go to the toilet; everybody sees you and knows which door you enter. Most people don't seem to give it a second thought.

When the waitress appears with the cigarettes, I ask her for a key to the restroom. You stir your coffee with a plastic spoon and keep silent. You don't ask for the key. Back from the restroom, I try to pass it to you.

"I don't need to go," you say.

"But a while back in the car . . . " I start.

"I don't need to go anymore."

You give me a puzzled look as if to say hey, you know how quickly you can lose the urge to piss, and I go along with your game. I know: you don't like being vulnerable. But you can't tell me you're comfortable using the women's toilet, knowing everybody would look at you in amazement, knowing the waitress would yell over the bar, "Hey young man, that's the lady's room." And you'd stiffen and say: "Yes, I know." If only there weren't so many men in the restaurant you'd simply use the men's room and there'd be no fuss and no mouths would drop in surprise. When needing to pee becomes such a problem, you prefer to stir your coffee and take no notice of the unpleasant details in life. Are you really convinced by your lies, I wonder, as I listen to you explain endlessly why you dislike our mutual acquaintance, Helen. It's her heavy makeup and how ridiculous she looks in women's clothes. When you stopped at her place for a cup of coffee she looked kind of scruffy. A type of woman you could never have sex with. I try to push aside the nagging thought of you having sex with her. I let it go by; after all, you always say how negative my take on everything is.

You search for a lighter. "Check your jacket," you say, holding an unlit cigarette between your lips.

"It's not here. You must have it."

You get up and search through your jeans pockets. You wear your jeans on your hips; the shirt sloppily hanging out at the waist. Only I know the breasts and nipples under this shirt, I realize with hidden delight. You look huge standing like this and frowning over a missing lighter. No wonder I feel so safe in your arms: you should never have sneaked so damn close to me.

You find three lighters in your pockets. You toss them on the table, sit down and light the cigarette. You shake your head in disbelief over your absentmindedness and look out of the window. You're thinking about something—but I'd rather not hear about it. Instead, you start telling me about some people I've never met. I don't know why you want me to know about them. Why you describe them to me, divide them into the good ones who do you favors and the bad ones who are hypocritical and ungrateful. It's as if you wanted to convince me how realistic your picture of them is—that your view isn't black-and-white and that you can judge people's characters even when I'm not around. Some of them like you very much, you say. They laugh at your jokes and appreciate how capable you are, how there's no work you can't handle. And you like to help them because you know that someday they'll return the favor. You, too, always return favors. "This is the right thing to do, right?" you say. I nod. Some women wonder why you never say anything personal about yourself. But you're not so stupid as to expose yourself, you're not a blabbermouth. I nod again. You never bore others with your problems. No, I think, you don't. You even spare yourself. I watch you talk, your hands drawing in the air the tales of favors done and returned. These darling hands. I don't need to concentrate on listening, you don't expect to hear my opinion—you don't want me involved. You talk incessantly and freely as there's nothing I could say about perfect strangers.

You've always talked about your school friends, people you worked with, relatives, about lots of things that are really irrelevant. Yet there was a time when I could imagine us in the background of those stories, I could imagine that you were talking about yourself, about me. But I don't feel this way now, not here in the restaurant where some women aren't given the key to the ladies' room. You want to bring us closer with stories of the people who've become your new selfish world.

"You're beautiful," I say.

I've interrupted you. You raise your eyebrows as if trying to guess what I *mean*. Gingerly, you smile. "What's the matter? What are you saying?"

"Nothing. Only what I see."

Don't be afraid of me. That's what I think but don't say.

You go on with your story. Suddenly, I feel I'm in a hole. Sitting next to you, looking at you, listening to you, sipping coffee on the road with you, and I can't believe I'm in a time hole. Don't move away from here, please. I don't say it, though. Let's stay here. If we leave, time will start running wild, swirling out of control, we'll be carried away. The time will disperse and it won't be the same swirl that'll take us away.

The words pulsate in my stomach. Yet I say nothing. You don't want to know. But you'll see. We'll be separated and I'll lose ground. When it happens you'll turn away.

"Let's go." You collect your wallet, cigarettes, and lighters. "What?" I don't know when you stopped talking or how your story ended. "Don't forget to take your jacket." Your hands tremble. Those darling hands. "Do you hear? Don't forget to take your jacket." Absorbed in thought I fold the jacket on my knees. You stand there looking at me. At last I get up, unfold the jacket and debate whether to put it on since it's cold outside. It pisses you off when I'm slow and absentminded, when I waste time on pointless tasks.

When I come out of the inn you've almost reached the car. You walk decisively and don't look back to see how closely I follow. It wasn't always like this. Why don't you ever look back anymore? You open the car door, take your shades out and put them on. Then you rest your elbow on the car roof and stare into the sun, your jeans hanging loosely off your hips. It's you who's in the time hole now. You understand now. You don't move and I'm scared stiff. You stand upright like a lion, dark hair shimmering in midday October sun. Then you take your shades off absentmindedly and wipe them on your shirt. I lean against the car roof, words throbbing on my lips.

"You're beautiful," I say again.

You don't want to listen. We get into the car. You light a cigarette and snivel. Putting the car in reverse, you place your hand on the back of my seat as if to embrace me. As if to embrace me—suddenly I know that you've been lying for a long time.

And that you'll have no piece of an apple strudel from the apples in the trunk.

"You're silly," you say as you shift into first. "You're just messing with me."

Why is nothing fun anymore? Why are you as deaf as a post?

By the time we reach the first turn you're engrossed in talking about a woman with a fantastic boyfriend. He really loves her and buys her kid sweets, but she's a stupid, spoiled cow who'll fuck him over sooner or later, you say. As if I'm supposed to be interested. Of course, you've already told her what she needed to be told, you've warned her. Needless to say, I don't know this cow. This is the kind of story you've been telling me. I don't want to understand that you're talking about yourself, about a woman who's your "cow."

About you being helpless.—I stop listening. I'm smoking and trying to open the window. I throw the butt out and take a deep breath. Secretly, I look at your profile. To steal a little more of you before many lonely months pass by and I completely forget how many days your period comes before mine. I light another cigarette and roll down the window again. That night at the *Central* when those roughs called you a bull dyke I watched you in profile too. You were so tediously calm, so damn calm. If they'd given you more shit when we passed them again, I would've kicked their teeth in. Because you never admit anything to yourself.

"You smoke too much," you say and go on with your stories.

My eyes engulf the white line separating the lanes. It disappears somewhere behind my back. That, I don't see. As if it won't be here anymore the next time I take this road home. As if only empty black asphalt will remain.

If you ever get married, I think in a frenzy, I won't come to the wedding. If you ever appear at my door with that thing dangling between your legs—I've told you once—I'll still love you. But I won't come to the wedding. Someday you'll have a child and you'll live a different life—or so you've told a friend of mine and asked her not to tell me. Don't worry. I too sometimes ignore the unpleasant details in life.

There's less and less of the white line to engulf. I put out the cigarette and sink into the seat as if it's going to get totally dark soon.

"Don't forget to switch on the headlights," I say. The silence has crept into the veins in my temples.

"You smoke too much," you say and go on drowning in the repetitive soap opera of your life.

. . .

I have a feeling that you won't pick me up on time, so I go alone to the disco on Sunday. It's there that I meet you. You arrive late and prattle on about where you've been, as if explanations and excuses still meant anything to either of us.

This is the first time we're together with your friends. You don't know I'm high from smoking dope. It makes me see so much more clearly how you fall into holes as if you were sliding into cracks between stairs in a restless sleep. I see you get lost in thought and fall silent for a moment, forgetting you're supposed to be boisterous and entertaining; I see you being pressured by self-deceptions. Please, run away from me, you bleed too much.

Hours later I have no idea where you are. At times I see you dance. You're drunk, but not too drunk. Sometimes I see you at the bar, laughing and—having forgotten a glass by the dance floor—ordering another beer. You don't forget to have fun, to pat people on their backs, make fun of transvestites in women's clothes, and holler hello to the passersby as if everyone's there because of you. I hide and watch you from dark corners, thinking how much I'd like to tell you the story of a man who was in love with a transvestite and ashamed of it. He finally took him to a restaurant for dinner. Everyone noticed they were both men. To make them leave early, the waiter made up a phony story about the table having been reserved. They left. As if they took no notice of the unpleasant details in other people's lives. The next day the man told his transvestite lover that he loved him and shot himself in the head.

This is precisely what it's like with us—in our local, Balkan version of the story. No Stonewall riots, of course; here we throw bottles at each other, here we live and nurse our own pathetic stories.—As if one of us has shot herself. Then you know that this blood can't be stopped anymore. No, no turning back for us this time.

Still sick from sucking in too much of the white line this afternoon, I shake my head no when someone asks if I want another beer. That was too much. I don't know whose head has split open and who is now banging against a bloodstained wall. Don't worry, I'll still bet that somewhere there's an open restroom for every one of us.

Translated by Mojca Šoštarko, revised by Beth Adler

THE SUBWAY

My friend Ines had prepared an exhibit of plans for a subway in Ljubljana. That's not actually her name, but I seem to prefer not to refer to her by her real name. Perhaps she'd prefer I not remember her at all. I've known Ines for a hundred years, but that doesn't mean much. Once we hitchhiked to Berlin together for a gay-and-lesbian festival and to Amsterdam for marijuana. But the Wall had fallen long ago and the part of the U-Bahn connecting West and East Berlin had been opened again. For an age of new possibilities. And some people were already venturing into undreamed-of dimensions.

Just as I was pondering whether we actually needed two stops as close together as Bavarian Court and Central Station, Ines came up to me. She was standing at the Star Park stop. Yes, I should add that this was an enormous exhibit, with a scale model taking up the entire floor space of the gallery and visitors walking among the tracks and stations, bending over to look at miniature buffets, Internet hubs, trees, and shops. Ines cleared her throat and put on a smile before thanking me for coming to see the exhibit, even though she hadn't been expecting me, which made it that much more of a surprise, and so on. Her pleasantries were meant to substitute for the invitation she hadn't sent, but fortunately I still sometimes browse through the culture section of the daily newspaper at the kitchen table while chewing my food. Oh, I'm so sorry, she said casually, you move so often that I can never keep up with your latest phone number, and you don't have a cell phone, of course. You've had all of my phone numbers, I thought, and you've never once bothered to call. To be conciliatory, though, I said that I didn't get out much anymore, but that I'd heard that her scale model really was interesting, so here I was and now finally I had a chance to look at and traverse all of Ljubljana in less than half an hour, ha, ha, ha. Ha, ha, ha, she replied in kind to my laughter, it was really nice of me to have come, my opinion meant a lot to her, this project really meant a lot to her, and for her part she was convinced that tonight she'd brought Europe to Ljubljana, even if only in the form of a scale model, ha, ha, ha—and that mattered more to her than anything else. I really agreed with her about that—a subway system was as good as Europe. Whenever I arrived in one of Europe's big cities and took the escalator down to the U-Bahn, the tube, or whatever, and drew that distinctive mixture of smog, gas fumes, and the filthy West in through my nostrils, deep into my lungs, I knew: This is Europe. Here I am, back in the place we call "there," where everything is supposed to be better and more interesting, or at least better labeled. I really like German U-Bahns, because despite what the signs say you can smoke practically everywhere. Or as you sprint from one line to the next, you can buy coffee in a plastic cup, stir sugar into it as you're climbing the stairs and, just before you get on the train, buy a slice of pizza or some similar take-out crap. Take-out, take-out, you can take anything out. And everything you can take out and eat in the endless draft of the subway is revolting, barely edible, greasy, and cheap. And all of it smells of the subway, all of it covered with the grime of the subway like a handkerchief that's been sneezed into. But that's the only place where I eat on the go—it's not done in Ljubljana. Ljubljana is my home and I know too many people and it's common knowledge that eating while you walk is bad for your stomach and nerves and skin and it makes you age faster. At home we don't hand a cookie to a guest, we offer them the whole open tin so they can pick one out for themselves—"straight out of the box." Ines's subway didn't have those smells or that grime or in the quieter evening hours those gray rats skittering among the tracks. Her subway was straight out of the box, with no dirty floors, no dog poop, no garbage or scraps of junk food. "They ought to clean all this up," she'd said to me years before at the Leopoldplatz station. "Smoking is a health risk for the other passengers. And the whole place is filthy and teeming with bums and junkies." At that time Ines was lesbian, but still her own person—neither a nutcase nor an addict nor a drunk—which made her want to clean everything up, so that the public and her parents wouldn't have to think that all queers and dykes were necessarily weirdos and drug addicts. And being an intellectual she knew she had to start with herself, shake off her illusions and unbridled aggression, get her degree, and do something for herself. And then sell that, of course. Then the Berlin Wall came down and the first things to get cleaned up were some lesbian and gay bars. But thank God in Ljubljana Ines wouldn't have to deal much with that problem, because here lesbians and queers cleaned themselves up for the most part and got out of the way. After our trip together to Prague, Ines quit being lesbian. She did send me one more picture postcard from Paris, where she was doing graduate work, and then she went polysexual or whatever.

"Does this . . . subway of yours have burek stands?" I asked Ines, since burek struck me as the only appropriate take-out food for chewing your way through the street scene of Ljubljana.

"No," she came to her project's defense without batting an eye. There'd be no bureks. "No greasy food at all, don't you see. We won't be selling any bureks. And at all the larger stations—for instance Bavarian Court, Central Station, Clinical Center, Šiška Cineplex— there'll only be stands with vegetarian fare. And fitness centers. I wouldn't even sell Coca-Cola—and I'm not going to allow any Benetton shops or Müller products."

"Do you mean those German Müller puddings? Those are the only ones I buy anymore."

"Yes, but they support really awful right-wing politics."

God knows what bureks support. Actually, Ines didn't support anything. She refused to dirty herself with politics.

"Smoking will be prohibited, of course, and we're taking that seriously. This is a clean project, you know what I mean, pure technology . . . well, I'll see you later," she said and went off to welcome a group of people dressed in black who'd gathered around the Triple Bridge station. I don't know why I briefly had the disagreeable feeling that she'd just poured cold water all over me. Of course she was excited, this was the opening of her first major project, which is why, as the rouge on her cheeks showed through the powder more and more, she was continually revolving around her stations, important university colleagues, prospective sponsors, and former loves.

It was apparent that a lot of people were interested in clean projects, pure technology, and pure art. I saw a few more familiar faces, but I preferred not to say hi to them, because I couldn't remember if I'd known them in high school or college. And no matter what I do, I can never remember who's married to whom and who's seeing whom on the side. Which is why it was easier to look at the floor—it even occurred to me how appropriate it was to have the exhibit on the floor so you didn't have to work to avoid acknowledging people—and stroll down the tracks. I reached the Rakovnik-Galjevica station, which was deserted. Maybe it wasn't so hard after all to look at your past from a distance, from a bird's-eye view, aloofly, lightly and in full. In that building there, which in the model was just a few hundred meters away from some steps leading down to the subway, I'd sat on the parquet floor packing my things. That was something I'd done in Ljubljana multiple times, but never, neither before nor after, as seriously and as thoroughly as I had that time on Galjevica. I suppose at least once in your life you have to pack all your stuff up down to the last scrap and leave, and after that it becomes a routine, all of your subsequent moves from one station to the next are a joke by comparison. It was amazing, I could have tacked some old photograph of mine, each dating to a different period, each with a different look, a different cause, at some different turning point in my life, featuring a different length and color of hair, with someone beside me, but most often not, to virtually every station in that model.

Ines and I liked taking pictures. In Prague we used up five rolls of film in just two days. We were constantly clicking our foolproof camera and getting the film developed. It didn't bother us in the slightest that the thing was broken, so that the worried owners of photo processing shops would hand us stacks of unfocused, double-exposed, inscrutable prints. We just acted as though we were experimenting with an avant-garde art form. Thus, one picture would have me standing right in the middle of the bell tower of a Prague church, while the next might show a streetcar passing through me. We'd howl in delight and grab the worst ones away from each other, as though we prized the shots that were most packed with disparate dimensions and the unlikeliest scenes. Because that's how we experienced Prague and all our other travels together. Whenever we saw a subway entrance, we'd barely glance at each other and then run down the stairs, since the tickets were so cheap. We'd also take pictures of each other in dark spaces, even though our camera could scarcely even manage the lengthening shadows of late afternoon.

"Ljubljana has to get a subway! Now I realize why I get so bored there, what I've been missing!" Ines said. Maybe that was the instant when she first got the idea of one day creating a plan for one, I don't remember. I couldn't focus on what she was saying, because the escalators down to the Prague subway stations were so steep that I didn't dare look all the way down or up, as it would make my head start to spin. Ines put her hands over my eyes and laughed at me. "That's those Russians for you, this is a regular space shuttle. You wouldn't make a very good astronaut, you're as lost as poor Laika."

Soon after that I really wasn't keeping up with Ines. No astronautical heights for me. I don't really know what went wrong, what separated the earth under our feet like an earthquake, so that several years later we were standing on totally different train platforms. Ines was already on her third car when I was just getting my first tattoo. I still had the impression we were traveling in the same directions, rushing up the same escalators and masticating similar take-out concoctions, we just weren't getting together that much anymore. Actually it hadn't been quite that clear-cut. From early on I'd looked the wrong way at a lot of things, the way I insisted on assembling and pasting disparate dimensions together, and that's why I'd never arrived at a proper project. In all those years we were together I'd never noticed that Ines was an astronaut and that she'd never be able to live and work as anything but that, and that—as she herself liked to announce—she'd find a way of landing her dreams so she could reach the heights with them. That's why she'd put a Ljubljana subway network on the floor, that's why she could stay bent over for hours on end, setting out stations and tracks and little cubes and, as she hovered over it all, thinking how clean and healthy it was under the ground she was standing on.

Then for a while I thought about how Ines had actually turned into a shrewd woman of the world, and somehow this change had escaped me. It escaped me when she began implementing her plan of actively adapting to her surroundings, something she'd talked about often. But it wasn't right for me to think that way, that's not how it was. Ines was just somebody else, though just who I'm not sure, since she was always someplace else, even when she was with me. Her dimensions were the thing that continually escaped me. Just that. Sure, she'd constantly told me that I was going to miss out on everything. But I didn't know how to live differently, nor did I want to. The way I was living seemed fine to me. I didn't know what was escaping me. And I still don't. I can't carry off a perfect bird's-eye view—which in any case would tell me too little about the scene underground.

Then my Ana arrived. At the door to the gallery she rose up on tiptoe, waved to me over the other guests' heads, and pointed to the bar. A few minutes later, beer in hand, she arrived at the Bežigrad station. I noticed Ines briefly looking her over through half-squinting eyes, as though she were trying to assess the state of completion of some project or other—just so nothing escaped her. Then she glanced over at me and gave me a satisfied smile, as though she already knew everything. I waved back. She came over and, before I'd even introduced them, reached a hand out to Ana. "I'm Ines, pleased to meet you," she said.

Ana smiled and said, "Are you the one who's involved in all the ambitious projects? You must have a lot of willpower." Then, saying she was going to head over to the Metelkova station, since that's where she spent most of her time anyway, Ana vanished down the tracks. Ines innocently asked me if that was my "new girl." It had immediately struck her that Ana had all the attributes (that's exactly the word she used) of a girlfriend of mine—under twenty-five, that lost look. Doubtless I was able to offer her on a platter all the life she didn't need. Ines was sounding like a drive-through psychiatrist from some American movie. Then, in a way that sounded good-natured, she added that I was probably paying too little attention to myself, which left me with too much spare time and a void that I filled with conflicted young girls, who later, when I settled down and was on my own for at least half a year, became grateful material for my stories. "That's right," I said, "You've got it exactly."

That made her angriest of all. It always got on her nerves whenever anyone agreed with her straight out. Ines didn't like it when people submitted to fate and sat with their arms crossed. She didn't like it when people ate food that was bad for them. Ines didn't like for people to do things she didn't like.

"You still know everything there is to know about girls and self-help, even though I'm sure you've long since forgotten . . . Oh, forget it," I said, and took a step in the direction of Metelkova.

"Aren't there just a lot of bums at Metelkova?"

"Even in your scale model?"

Ines turned to the first passersby and began talking to them. I felt as though she'd left me far away from herself, from everyone, back in that former dead end of the subway between East and West Berlin, where there were only armed East German soldiers standing, looking like unreal shadows from the world on the far side of the wall.

At the Metelkova station Ana put her arm around me and teasingly said, "What do you say, my dearest bum, shall we get out of here?"

I kissed her, more in confusion than on purpose, and wondered why I always locked horns with Ines. As though something weren't right. As though both of us, Ines and I, were standing in the wrong place and trying to convince each other that a right place existed somewhere.

"I don't know," I said absently, "I don't know, Ana, let's walk around some more, bring me a beer and let's walk around some more . . ."

"Fine," she said, and went for the beer. I thought maybe I'd offended her by not wanting to go. Once she'd chided me for getting distracted in groups of people and forgetting about her. It's true. All those dimensions. I can't track them all, I can't patch them together into a neat bundle.

I wanted to walk by myself. I wanted to walk past all the stops where I'd lived at one time or another. Once a friend advised me to get on my bike and ride past all the houses and apartment buildings in Ljubljana where I'd once lived. Physical auto-reflection, they called it. And then, once back home, I actually sat down at my desk and wrote out a long list of all the addresses in chronological order. I spent a long time thinking about how to make my pilgrimage among all those life stations—should I observe the chronological sequence of my moves or should I base it on the geographical proximity of one domicile to another? This latter would be easier, of course, but at the expense of the full experience of auto-reflection. Then I made some calculations: how much time would it take if I bicycled from one address to the next, based on the chronological order of my moves? It turned out that I'd have to get up at about six in the morning in

order to finish tracing my life's succession of moves by roughly
eight in the evening. In the end I didn't set out on that trip.
My friend's idea was a good one, I have to admit, but much
harder to carry out. Ultimately it was Ines's plan for a subway
in Ljubljana that made a ten-minute cartographic tour of all my
former addresses in chronological order possible: Hrastje, the
Triple Bridge, Bežigrad II, Rožna dolina, Trnovo, Rožna dolina,
Bežigrad II, Novo Polje, Rakovnik-Galjevica, Bežigrad I . . .

"Let's go, I want to go, let's go home and watch a movie," Ana
said precisely at the moment when I was thinking about walking
through all of my stops in reverse order. But that would've been
regression, so it was a good thing that we left.

"Are you going already?" Ines called out.

I nodded to her from the doorway, casting a final glance at
the model of the subway. Then my Ana put her arm around me.
My Ana, my stations, my Ljubljana, my Europe, my geography.

TRANSLATED BY MICHAEL BIGGINS

LETTERS FROM A PRISONER

When Nada left me I wanted to kill myself. One summer evening when the city was at its most enjoyable, she invited me out for coffee. But an invitation to coffee in the evening, with its implicit threat of a swift end to the meeting, couldn't bode well. We sat in a deserted café alongside the Ljubljanica River. As she took too quick a sip of the overly hot coffee, swore and set her cup down, I noticed her hands were shaking. "You know . . . ," she began without looking at me. I nodded distractedly, although naturally I didn't want to know any of what was to follow. In a single breath she told me that she wanted to break off our occasional trysts, and in the process she paused only long enough to cool her scalded tongue. Well, we could still get together for drinks and a chat, she hurried to add, but she wouldn't be coming to my house anymore. She thought I was a fine person, one of the best she'd ever known, but she couldn't be with me anymore. She was afraid she might fall in love, and she didn't want that, because then both of us would suffer. She was just stretched too thin, in too many directions. There were too many women around her. Not that they meant anything to her, but it would inevitably be hurtful to me to know she was intimate with them. In short, she loved me so much that she had to leave me. Then she wanted me to see her home, but as the offended party I insisted that she get up first and leave, if that's what she'd decided. That I didn't need any consolation for idiots. She got up and hugged me. When she tried to kiss me, I turned my head away. Nada the stretched-too-thin was gone, but I still had my head turned aside and was looking down at the water.

Of course there's no evidence left of my pathetic intention to kill myself, because I didn't tell anyone about it. I had some real friends who'd have wrung my neck if they'd known what black thoughts I'd succumbed to, and such a fine person at that. At the same time they were all convinced that Nada wasn't worthy of me, that, frankly, she was a common flirt and bullshitter who had the emotional intelligence of a high schooler. And if I could just get over my infatuation, my friends thought, I'd realize quite quickly that my beloved and I had absolutely nothing to talk about.

Indeed, it would've been hard for me to admit that life didn't seem worth it anymore without Nada. You kill yourself when the stock market crashes, or you go into debt, or your two-story house burns down to the ground. All right, you can also kill yourself when you lose your mind. But none of these things had happened to me. I'd only been left by a girl who wasn't quite right upstairs. And was a little too young for me. So why should I want to kill myself once she was gone? We did have one subject in common. The sex was good, the best I'd ever experienced. But that I should do away with myself on account of a bothersome ache between my legs made the least sense of all. And so, once again, I was forced to survive. In spite of the lonely evenings when I refused to go out to the teeming cafés on the banks of the Ljubljanica, so I wouldn't have to see with my own eyes Nada practicing her art of being stretched too thin among too many women. Of course, of course, to some extent I also hoped she'd miss me once we stopped seeing each other, that she'd come to her senses and one fine evening show up at my door and confess that she'd made a terrible mistake by not letting herself fall in love with me. Because she simply couldn't live without me.

While I waited for that perpetually retreating evening of Ana's imaginary contrite return, I also put off killing myself. I spent the hot summer nights, which no one in town is able to spend completely alone, lying in bed, unsuccessfully trying to drive away thoughts of the void left by Nada's departure. But that was precisely what I wanted to think about, and only about that. When I thought of her kissing me, I'd get up and make myself coffee to stop the tears from welling up. When I closed my eyes and felt the shadow of her touch, I'd light up a cigarette to slow down my quickening pulse. And when I shifted in my chair from the imaginary weight of her body, I went into my roommate's empty room and scanned the shelves full of books. My roommate had been studying abroad for over a year, during which time I was free to make use of her private library at will. That summer I read a tremendous amount. I thought that if I read all of the Nobel Prize winners assembled in her library, Nada would invite me back out for coffee, even if only to tell me she was leaving me again. But after a few days' intensive reading I calculated that my chances were better if I focused on the Hundred Novels series, because I'd already read a lot of those books for assignments in high school, while others of them I'd read just for fun. I'd sit in her room, calculating how many books I had left to read in this or that series. Just as I was coming to the surprising conclusion that my chances were best with the Condor series, the front doorbell rang. I ran down the stairs, preparing myself to be disappointed. In fact I was curious just who could've had me so much in mind that summer evening that they decided to visit. But it turned out to be Nada, after all. Precisely the way I'd wished her to be in my fondest daydreams: slightly timid, out of breath—which told me she'd ridden her bicycle at top speed to get there—her eyes bloodshot. In short, desperate and contrite. As though fate itself were standing at my door. She hugged me as I stood there numb, my arms hanging down at my sides. Until she grabbed onto me like a drowning person who's glimpsed a chance of being rescued at the last moment, which struck me as terribly moving. I thought to myself: Fine, I'll hug her and maybe even kiss her, but I'm not playing at anything more. Yet a few minutes later, when we were sitting in my room and had opened a bottle of wine, I very quickly began doing what I didn't want to play at. But I felt that there must be something very special between us.

While making coffee for breakfast next morning, I thought about how there was no need to take things so tragically and dramatically, since I could after all enjoy the very best she had to offer and leave the bad things to others. When I brought the coffee into the bedroom, Nada was fully dressed with the headphones of the Walkman she was always listening to on her bike already around her neck. The room filled instantly with dark premonitions. Nada's discomfort was back with full force. She didn't want to hurt me again, she babbled at my bedroom door, but she also couldn't go on without me completely. She couldn't get me out of her head, even if this was hurtful to both of us. The fact that she used the word "us" particularly annoyed me, because I'd reserved the right to any real pain exclusively for myself. I'd better not count on anything changing now, she added, and what's more, it'd be very risky if she fell in love with me. She'd always be afraid of that happening and I'd better not forget how susceptible she was to strong feelings for me. She didn't forget to emphasize that sex with me had been incredible, something that others couldn't compare to, and that nobody else was half as good. Because I was such a wonderful person and she only wanted to give me the very best. But because she couldn't do that anymore, she needed to be honest and go. That evening I spent hugging my knees in my chair next to an open window. Both cups of coffee from morning still stood there, untouched. I derived pleasure from staring at what, clearly, neither one of us dared to drink to the end.

Over the following days I became even more convinced that I couldn't go on living. As before, I didn't call up a single friend to share that I'd reached an even greater depth of despair on account of that unworthy Nada. In the evenings I'd torture myself fantasizing that we were making love in my bed. I took my blanket and moved to my roommate's room, where I lay down in front of her personal library. Now none of the book series looked promising to me. Even if I did read one of them in its entirety, did I really still have the heart for another of Nada's anti-professions of love?

It was no good. All I wanted was to cease to exist. That would've been good news for Nada. I took pleasure in imagining Nada crying and pulling her hair out while her friends kept a close watch to keep her from doing herself in, too, since with me gone her life would inevitably lose all meaning. What would be the point of nursing those noble feelings toward me if I was no more? What point in going on and being stretched thin, if I'd been the only really good one, the very best, and nobody else was a hundredth as good?

As I daydreamed about the positive effects of my death, my eyes fixed blankly on a cardboard shoe box marked "Letters." I rose mechanically and reached for the box, which was on a middle shelf. Other people's letters are always interesting, even to suicides. The slightly yellowed envelopes addressed to my roommate for the most part had uninteresting contents. Letters from her worried parents dating to her college years, letters from friends back home who missed her and faithfully relayed stacks of trivial information, a letter from a fiancé she'd never mentioned to me, picture postcards from vacations to eternally identical coastal towns. At the very bottom were envelopes addressed in a careful, respectful hand, which contained sheets densely covered with writing. At first I just glanced through them, but when I picked up words like "prison," "entirely on my own," "thoughtlessly pacing the prison courtyard," and "the senselessness of our lives," curiosity got the better of me and I began reading the thick letters from the beginning. The author of the letters was a prisoner whom my roommate had gotten to know in the course of conducting interviews of prisoners as part of her research for a term paper. From that time on, apparently, he'd continued regularly to write her long letters. At the end of each letter he went on at length about his past, because he wanted her to understand why he'd landed in jail and what in his life's experience had led him to theft, burglary and, ultimately, violence.

He always titled the confessional part of his letters "My Life's Story." He started by describing an incident from childhood when he bit his grandmother's leg, and she in her drunkenness literally threw him over a fence into a pigpen. From that time on he spent a lot of time with pigs and was even convinced that he ultimately learned their language, except that now he no longer had anyone he could oink with. From that time on the members of his depraved peasant family would at least leave him alone as long as he was spending time with the pigs. In another letter he expressed his outrage and disappointment at his sentence, at being thrown in the slammer, as he put it, for almost five years. As part of his life's story he described his first romance with a girl when he was growing up in the country. She was his uncle's stepdaughter, a vivacious blue-eyed girl who always teased him by saying he should watch out, because all blue-eyed girls were deceitful in love. He didn't believe her. Then, when he caught her with her stepfather, his uncle, out in a field, his world came crashing down. As it would do over and over again after that. It was no use when the blue-eyed girl came begging him to listen to her, to marry her and save her from his uncle. One afternoon he was out tending the cows and mourning for his lost love. When the blue-eyed girl came to him in tears, trying to kiss him, he was furious and threw her into a nearby stream. From that day on she went every day to swim and sing in that stream, and her uncle wouldn't touch her anymore, because she had no appeal for him soaking wet.

During the day I'd torture myself with thoughts of Nada, while saving the prisoner's letters for nighttime. One evening I discovered something unusual. To my amazement and delight, at the bottom of the shoe box there were at least a dozen of the prisoner's letters that my roommate hadn't even opened. When I opened the first one, it was immediately clear to me that she'd stopped writing to him. Following some accusations that she'd dumped him, he wrote her about his day-to-day life, about how he didn't even have money for cigarettes, that he'd been in a fight with some Croat who was an alcoholic, and so on. This part I read perfunctorily; what I was really looking forward to was the next chapter of his life's story. In this letter he'd reached his high school apprenticeship years, when he wanted to become an automobile painter. When the supervisor of his workshop fired him for the innocent theft of some candles, he took his revenge in blind fury. One night he crept up behind the supervisor's house, which was next door to the workshop, climbed over the fence, and threw the dog, which knew him and didn't bark, a piece of poisoned meat. The dog, which incidentally liked him a lot, began writhing in pain, and at that point he jumped back over the fence and ran down the pitch-dark road back into town. As he heard the dog howling in pain, tears streamed down his face and he swore he'd never let anyone abuse him again.

The next day I didn't wake up until noon. I couldn't stop thinking about the prisoner's almost prophetic-sounding, yet threatening words about how by poisoning the dog he was so fond of he'd put an end to his abuse, that obscure concept he mentioned so often in his letters. I cleaned the apartment, fixed some lunch, and showered. I was determined to put an end to my exile and rejoin the world. I took a walk along the Ljubljanica, casually lighting up cigarettes and acting as though an evening stroll like this were the most ordinary thing in the world for me. In fact I was looking for anyone I knew whom I could sit down and join, while cautiously sizing up every woman who walked by for signs that she might be part of the orbit in which Nada was stretched too thin. As it began to get dark, I stopped at a café for something to drink, taking a seat on a bench by the river and away from people. I thought about the prisoner's blue-eyed girlfriend, who might to this day be going for swims in the stream. Then I heard some familiar voices. Across from my hidden corner under the trees three women were approaching the café. When they sat down at a table, I recognized Nada among them. My first thought was of escaping, but I couldn't move and wasn't for anything in the world going to let them notice me on my lonely bench under the tree. My eyes were riveted to Nada, who in company was always the loudest, constantly laughing at her own jokes. She filled her friends' glasses, let slip a couple of double entendres while lighting their cigarettes, scanning the vicinity nervously all the while. Soon two more women I didn't know approached their table. Nada greeted them noisily, hugging and kissing them. I was so consumed with curiosity about which of them she might be attracted to that I couldn't move. Nada thrived in the company of women, but she never stopped anxiously looking around, as though seeking out new objects of interest. When one of them suggested that they take their beers and move to a bench by the water, I leaped off mine and hurried away. They didn't notice me.

Once home I immediately opened the shoe box and began reading a new, previously unopened letter from the prisoner. But the voices and boisterous laughter of Nada and her friends, laced with the sound of the river, still echoed in my ears, even if it did fade away as I retreated homeward. For an instant I was so angry I could've flung them all in the Ljubljanica. I stopped even thinking of how I wished I could just die. The reason was simple—I knew I could go out every evening and enjoy myself while lurking on that bench under the tree . . .

In one of his last letters the prisoner again threatens to stop writing my roommate, because it's been years since he'd encountered this much shamelessness. He was more than convinced that she was still reading his letters. He mentioned that she could come visit him sometime and bring something along—not money, he didn't want that, just some little treat. In his life's story he recalled his brothers and sisters, whom he otherwise mentions nowhere among the many chapters about his childhood. Of course they were estranged from each other, they'd never understood him and he'd always been the family outcast. They were ashamed of him long before he landed in prison. But he knew that was only because he saw through all their dirty secrets. His oldest sister worked in a hospital as a nurse supervisor, but she'd been susceptible to bribes from early on. So once he swiped all her cash from her and went for the first time to a casino—at age seventeen—but that didn't teach her that sooner or later ill-gotten money will dry up. His youngest brother had always been a sweet, curly-haired child who had the whole village eating out of his hand. But he was also a sickly little brat, a fact that no one was willing to recognize, a louse who used his sweet, innocent face to blame his own misdeeds on others. Of course, it was only the prisoner-to-be who was aware of that, so he gave his sweet little brother a few good knocks on the sly, since it was obvious he needed to be punished—but the punches only made him cuter and more devious. His middle brother was the town drunkard, no more, no less. People always see drunkards as basically kind people who've made nothing of their lives, except that the reason they're failures is that they're so damned oversensitive. Which isn't right. Just as it wasn't right for everyone to grab him under the arms and drag him from the pub back home. One evening the family sent him to fetch his drunken brother. He ran into him when he was already halfway home. He hoisted him up over his shoulder and dragged him back down the dark country road, listening to his incoherent blather and his groundless abuse, which always ended in a sudden gush of vomit. His drunken brother was like a fountain that alternately gurgled up curse words, disgusting whimpers, unfocused anger, and bits of half-digested food. Once he slid his shoulder out from under his brother's heavy arm, just to see if unsupported he really would stagger into a ditch. In actual fact, he rolled so far down the steep hillside into the forest that it took three days for them to find him. While all the others were mourning his loss, only the future prisoner thought that at least one of them had learned his lesson.

The next evening I was perched back on the bench across from the café. Either I got there late or the women had arrived early. All of them had already said their goodbyes to Nada, who stubbornly remained sitting alone at their table. I felt heartened by the fact that since her friends' departure the two of us were left alone in some way, although she didn't know that. I was hoping she'd keep anxiously looking around, particularly if I turned out to be the missing object of her anxiousness. Then Nada's face melted into a smile that soon after changed into an expression of contrived displeasure. One of her friends who'd left her prematurely was coming back to the table. She was the quietest and most unobtrusive of the three, and also the one Nada addressed the least, so she must have been a good listener.

"I'm not playing this game anymore," the quiet woman said in a surprisingly assertive voice. Nada didn't so much as twitch in response. Her defensive posture got on my nerves.

"You keep doing that!" she went on. "Are you happy now that you're sitting here by yourself? Don't think I'm going with you now. I've told you already any number of times, things between us aren't the way you think."

"What way are they, Lidija?" Nada asked, now on the offensive.

Previously invisible Lidija picked up Nada's hand in her own and explained to her solicitously, as you might to an emotionally traumatized child, that she should have no illusions about a serious relationship. That what they had was nice in its own right, but anything more would just cause problems, because love was too risky a thing. It was like a drug that you can't stop taking before it sucks you in completely and then you have to try to get over the person. And it made no sense, in fact it was wrong to have to get over people who mean so much to you. Lidija ended by assuring Nada that she meant a great deal to her, too much for her to risk falling in love. The whole time she spoke in shameless, simplified sentences that would've been impossible to contradict. I had to admit: Lidija's oral delivery was incomparably better than Nada's.

A few evenings later I put the cardboard box with its letters all read back on its shelf and returned to the books. Elsewhere on my roommate's bookshelves I'd discovered quite an obscure series consisting of lesser-known works by otherwise prominent authors. To my bitter delight I discovered that this was the shortest series of all, so that within a very short time I had the final, tenth book in hand. The author oscillated between a confessional memoir and a traditional *Bildungsroman*. But some of the passages were nicely, if not brilliantly executed. For instance a chapter about how he'd lived a large part of his childhood among pigs and learned how to oink. His first love, a blue-eyed country girl who in a fury of disenchantment had thrown herself into a stream. And the senseless revenge he exacted on his boss by poisoning the man's dog, which he was so fond of. He behaved even worse toward his brothers and sisters, accusing them all of deceit, greed, and drunkenness, and arrogating the right to himself to teach them life lessons. I knew the episodes down to the finest detail, having read almost every chapter already in the excerpts from the prisoner's life.

I put the last book of the shortest series back on its shelf, but the doorbell remained silent.

TRANSLATED BY MICHAEL BIGGINS

PROCULIN

Moving fast toward the railway station restroom I go through my pockets feverishly: two packs of cigarettes, a lighter, some cash, a monthly bus pass, spare elastic cord for my ponytail, face powder, poppers, hair gel—everything's here. There's no stopping me now, I could do just about anything. There's no need to rush, though. I have plenty of time to execute my little plan comfortably.

Once in the restroom I position myself in front of the first of a line of mirrors and empty my pockets. Following the established routine, I carefully arrange all my little dependencies on the shelf above the sink. Then I look in the mirror and check my eyes. They're red from fatigue, from the shock of the telegram that's so abruptly ended the drowsy slumber I indulged in for weeks. Proculin first, then.—And I came so close to believing that nothing could wake me up anymore, that nothing could lure me out into the unprotected crush of the daily grind.

A large number of Proculin drops later I raise my head and close my eyes in a short meditation, waiting for the initial sharp tingling sensation to wear off. As always, I let the biting Proculin tears run down my cheeks leaving that self-sufficient feeling of having just had a good, well-deserved cry that stays with me for minutes. How many good cries have I really had up to now? Whenever I use Proculin I try to think of "the three best cries of my life." It must be my thirty-odd years getting at me, but I can't say with certainty what's brought me the most sorrow in life. I realize with horror that I don't recall hard times as well I used to. Nothing seems to be worth genuine sorrow any more. Teardrops suggest inexperience, childishness, selfishness, Proculin even.—What about the time when my grandfather died? Only two hours after the funeral I forgot about having cried at all and was playing with other children in the village. Why is there no time to cry when you're a child? What about that time in the fifth grade when I was symbolically kicked out of class by a group of schoolmates who arrogated the authority to decide who was to be liked and who disliked. Yes, I did cry then, but that was stupid, that cry was a mistake. No, no, it must've been something that happened much later . . . But when? I seem to remember well the feeling, a true, deep and gripping sorrow, yet I can't think of the exact moments when I felt it. Did it have to do with love? Love is supposed to hurt the most.—When you get up before me in the morning and walk around the room like an animal just released from chains after what's been ages. An animal that doesn't believe it can go freely now. Because running away is all you know. You put on a T-shirt and roll a joint, believing that this took you long enough to do instead of the unuttered goodbye. Searching your jacket for paper handkerchiefs, you already put the cigarettes back in your pocket. You have nothing to say to me. I hold your hand—do you want a cup of coffee—but it's as cold as lizard's skin. I can't bear to tell you about my nightmares now, to be a stone in your arms. I swear to myself that I'll cry out loud when you close the door behind you. Maybe then I'll be able to lean over small chasms and poke into souls. But all I do is wonder where you've run away to. Why do you love your chains so much? How far would my shouts reach? Still, the whole thing wasn't as sad as it was tedious.

End of meditation. I lean forward and almost touch the mirror with my nose; I open my eyes wide. After another dose of Proculin they're even more bloodshot than before, but the treacherous tiny veins slowly retract from the natural whiteness of my eyeballs. A few more drops in an hour or so and I won't need any more until morning. Proculin works miracles.

It's one of the few products that truly help you get through everyday stress. A little, yet effective trick. Like face powder. For a while it conceals unsightly acne and skin complaints in intimate light. Some types of lipstick cover even minor cold sores. Little tricks that can change so many things, sometimes even gender, and make them better. I put the drops, face powder, lipstick, cigarettes and lighter back into my pockets—the lower right-hand one being reserved for the lighter. For a few seconds I'm pleasantly excited by the smell of poppers. One more look in the mirror to check my profile. I did a good job with the face powder. I'm finally happy with my profile, which also might be a consequence of my mature age. When you gradually lose your critical attitude about what can't be changed or corrected. And praise the transitory nature of things.

I proceed along the railway tracks toward the bar at the corner that serves truly horrible coffee. Suddenly, I feel weak. I haven't eaten today, yet the thought of food makes my mouth water. In passing I say hello to three men whose names I don't even know, and hasten my pace as if in a hurry to get to the platform. I'm no longer keen on talking to almost perfect strangers.

This is my third cup of coffee and the second glass of Schweppes today. I'm out of luck. The train is arriving on time and it'd take a miracle to hear it announced as not running today. Another five minutes and I'll be off to platform No. 3. I itch to do something.—I've exhausted my ideas for keeping my mind busy. When the train makes its way past the platform, whistling, I feel like rushing down the stairs and simply running away. My God, I don't know what I'm doing.

The train comes to a halt. Seeing the first passengers get off I feel uneasy, almost panicky. The train is almost empty; still I hope to see an omen that might deter me from waiting. Like somebody wearing a black hat.—Once, years ago, at the same time of the year I was in London. In the soothing, big city bustle of races, colorful clothes, and wailing sirens I was upset by my first lover's quarrel. I was about twenty-four, twenty-five. Years of age.—Emptiness all around.

An elderly couple with tears in their eyes is hugging a suit-case-laden girl, must be an architecture or design student back from advanced training at a university in England. I used to toy with the idea of going to study in England; no doubt some subject that'd be of no use here, but for that I'd need a busload of friends to lend me a hundred dollars each. The promising architect is joined by a typical nuclear family of four. The father, still on the train, is handing down suitcases—careful, glasses— to the mother and the children already on the platform. Each time he bends his trousers creep up to his mid-calves showing two crossed tennis rackets stitched on his snow-white socks. The children too are wearing tennis socks. When the tennis team collects its luggage and—where's the cab—marches toward the exit, I'm left alone. I realize I'm trembling uncontrollably.

She gets off the train last, possibly hoping to shatter my potential disappointment in grand style. I really didn't want her to come. I didn't want to go through the same conversations, the same attempts to persuade and battles lost in advance, not her, no. Even having to do this last deal with her was too much.— Just yesterday I combed all through my closet. I felt no regret throwing out all the shirts I'd never worn, the jackets saved for some costume party, the moth-infested black socks. And I gave no thought to donating them to charity. I just dumped everything in the bathtub and soaked it in bleach. Then I filled several big black trash bags and carried them to the dumpster. When my shirts and vests and socks get to a landfill they'll be white, beautifully white.

No more deep tasting of mouths, no bland goodbyes, no catlike shame of the eyes looking at her sweaty scalp, no light-hearted meetings by day. None of it. None of that crap any more.

She brings her face closer for a kiss and I recoil as if suddenly embarrassed to be seen kissing in public. She gives me a cynical smile. How come I didn't start to hate her before?

Not a word exchanged, we walk toward the restroom, her arm deliberately tucked under mine. I can't be bothered to pull away. By the time we get into a toilet stall it's gotten dark. I think

I'm crying. The rivers in me have broken loose. If I could I'd tell
about them. I say I'm cold, more to myself than to her really, and
I wipe my nose.—I could also have punched her.

I pass her the packet with bottles of poppers and, without
counting, take a roll of Deutschmarks in return. She too refuses
to check the package and puts it in her inside jacket pocket. "I
trust you," she murmurs. "Not that I care," I place my hand on
the door handle, "this is our last time together."

"Last time together? You mean our last deal or our last ren-
dezvous?" "Both." She falls silent. Searching for words outside
her usual repertoire. This is no time to bluff. I enjoy watching
her struggle. "But you're the only woman I do business with,
you're the only one I can trust. We should support each other,
forgive one another. Together we could do just about anything!"

"Support each together, right. To hell with that!" I open the
door. She grabs me by the hand and slams the door shut.—My
ears hurt. The sound vibrates like the echo of my footsteps along
the pavement in front of a funeral chapel when I was five or six
years old and had sneaked past the entrance to take a peek at a
dead neighbor while my grandmother was planting pansies on
my grandfather's grave. Once inside, I stepped onto the bench
behind the mourners and pressed my nose against a glass pane,
eagerly curious; how can you tell from looking at the body that
the person has died of insanity? A gravedigger chased me away
and I ran all the way to my grandfather's grave. My grandmother
had no respect for people who failed to grasp the eloquent gran-
deur of death. "Such people aren't cut out to be gravediggers,"
she murmured, and added that this particular gravedigger
should be forced to eat his dead if he was going to deny others
the chance to see them . . . What if the gravedigger ate up the
neighbor's insanity together with her dead body? "Grandma,
how does it show on a corpse that a person has died of insanity?"
"Be still, child, as I'm about to finish planting pansies. They're
not too promising this year. You know nothing about life, child.
Dead people can't be insane, their brains are gone."

Let me out of this stall, for God's sake, let me out. I say, "I can't go on like this. I'm tired." "Yes," she tries to be conciliatory and understanding. "Your eyes are red. I'm taking you out for a pizza. I need to sit and eat beside you. I want it, you can't deny me that. I love you." How wild my rivers rage.

I keep on kicking the door but it won't yield under her firm grip. I start pounding instead and disbelieve the tears running down my cheeks. Why, who is it that I'm crying for? I squeeze her arm, "Let go . . . That's enough."

Back at the mirror, between drops of Proculin, I glance occasionally toward what I hope is a firmly closed stall. I've removed the door handle. No blood has trickled out from under the door. Maybe people don't bleed that much after all. Maybe they don't hurt that much. Not that I want to know. After all, I did wrap my pullover around her neck. To stop the crimson red opening on her tanned neck from bleeding. Tanned neck? It should be white, bluish or ashen. Or . . . I don't want to know. Through the Proculin film, which burns the clarity of my eyes, I look for changes in my reflection, for traces of pallor or drawn features. I don't know. If the rivers are raging. My hands are trembling, yet I won't ascribe any importance to the tears shed in the stall. I'll disregard them completely.

The roll of Deutschmarks in my pocket should get me at least to Budapest and back. I'll be able to go shopping. For clothes. I'll go to the airport. All the traveling I've done. The hours spent at airports, recorded nowhere, persist in my memory.—Once I was so tired that I fell asleep across the chairs in a lounge and dreamed about a white flame consuming the building. I woke up with the sun beaming onto my face through a large terrace window, amazed at the countless faces staring at me. I realized they were looking out of the window and watching planes landing and taking off. Children gesticulated with their arms spread out like wings and pointed their fingers at the overheated glass panes . . . I was shocked at how little I knew about life.

My hands trembled in an attempt to close the switchblade. I

shoved it into my inside jacket pocket, the torn one I no longer
regard as a pocket. How had I managed to reach into it and pull
out the knife in what must have been seconds?

My face has turned white. Something's telling me it shouldn't
be like this. Yet it shouldn't be any different either. I could love
her, love her very much. But these are nothing but words now.

. . .

Not much has changed since. I moved house about four years
ago. Not that my old house had burned down or anything. I
have tattoos now. In front of a mirror, after I arrange all my
dependencies on the shelf, I always check their color and oil
them, line after line, letter after letter.—Then I question myself
in earnest. But what can I tell—paralyzed for a moment? I don't
laugh much. Because I ask myself how many pitiful, ignoble
mishaps, charming quandaries, little lies,

how many wrong steps,

twitching of pupils—

Proculin drops—

how many slips of the tongue

are still needed. To make it work. For instance: I raise my
hands up to my neck and squeeze. I empty the skull of its expres-
sionless eyeballs and once and for all rescue it from the rolling
splinters of my straw childhood. All this in front of a railway
station mirror itself pushed to a soft whiteness—because nobody
else will get to know me enough.

TRANSLATED BY MOJCA ŠOŠTARKO

TRIPS ARE CHEAPER NOW, TOO

She sent her a postcard, a last-minute note before New Year's. "Come on, it's okay! I'm expecting you, as we've arranged! Yours, Jana." Sure, she wrote other things as well, so many, actually, she almost ran out of space; but they weren't that important. She hurried to the post office and dropped the tacky picture of a Christmas tree in the mailbox—there was really no time to shop around for anything in better taste—all that mattered was that the note arrive in time, as soon as possible. As the green-gold Christmas tree slid under the red flap and disappeared soundlessly into the full mailbox, Jana felt her day had come to a fairly satisfactory end. After all, she'd been under considerable pressure, she'd had less than twenty minutes to buy the post-card, write it, and mail it. Only then could she make her way to her apartment along the now too familiar route, looking at the Christmas decorations through the low windows, eyeing the infrequent passersby. Perhaps now she was no longer so utterly alone, so forgotten in a foreign city. The day felt somehow differ-ent. She dropped her cigarette in the snow, it really was too cold to smoke, she put on her new gloves and shoved her hands deep into her shallow pockets. "Ugh," she shivered with the cold and even smiled at herself, not sourly as was her habit, but wisely and with resignation, as though she knew that the postcard in the mailbox was not the best of moves in her life. She could always tell them in advance, these not-the-best-of-moves in her life, and she always knew just when it would be too late. Then she waited until it really was too late.

When Vivi walked in through Jana's door three days later

without having received the note on the reverse side of the tacky Christmas tree that, naturally, couldn't have been the best of possible outcomes. But Jana refused to let it bother her; she'd busied herself decorating the apartment, she'd also washed the bed linen the day before their encounter so that it would smell fresh, she'd stacked the presents on the nightstand on Vivi's side of the bed . . . It all goes together somehow, she thought moments before she heard the taxi stop outside her building, everything matched, including the color of the wrapping paper on the gifts and the bedclothes and the ceiling with the silver painted stars. Even the bottle of champagne was suitably blue with a silvery design. She'd really made an effort, and because she was aware how stupid one felt when in time it all turned out to have been futile, Jana always tried very hard not to let it all become futile.

Vivi had no Christmas presents for Jana, not a single one. Vivi had only brought herself, because Jana had insisted. Jana, naturally, didn't say anything at the time; for half an hour she pretended that they were just having coffee and chatting after having been separated for several months, and that everything else wasn't yet important. Then she popped to the store for some cigarettes, and when she returned in something like three-and-a-half minutes, they briefly recounted the most outstanding events of their separate lives and went to the bedroom, where Vivi handled the gifts and said that she liked them the way they were and that she wouldn't open them just yet. Because Vivi had no energy left for joy. And then it was already time for a joint and Jana wanted to have peace while she was getting stoned, she didn't want to think about the presents she never received, since such downbeat thoughts could spoil her mood. And that wouldn't do. It simply wasn't the right time to be crabby—not yet. Jana knew well enough that she'd recall this unpleasantness with the presents later, perhaps several months or even a year later, oh yes, she'd remember it often and she wouldn't forgive Vivi for what shouldn't be forgotten, and already now

Jana relished the prospect. "You don't know what she was like," she'd tell her friends in the future, "you have no idea, she didn't even bring me a Christmas present though we hadn't seen each other in such a long time. And I was so blindly caring I gave her several presents, of course . . ." Now, however, was really not the right moment, Jana didn't want to be petty now because that would've immediately prompted Vivi to ask whether she really liked feeling sorry for herself so much. As a matter of fact, she did; Jana genuinely liked feeling sorry for herself. Yuletide would often find her strolling along the streets of Utrecht alone, following with her eyes the cyclists apparently immune to colds. She'd unabashedly stare through the uncurtained windows at the people sitting amid tinsel and other kitsch and watching television, chatting, or dropping off in their armchairs in a film-like version of wintertime idyll. Walking, Jana would draw up a mental list of everything she lacked, such as a sense of security, a warm home, a shelter, close friends around her; she no longer had a home even back home in Slovenia because she always just lived here or there . . . She called this list of things lacking in her life her "merry list," probably in relation to Christmas. She was incapable of just plopping herself down in an easy chair in the afternoon, carefree, and dozing off only to wake up at sweet dusk. "When dusk falls, we'll . . ." her family used to say when she was little, so in addition to Christmas, winter dusk would also tug at her heartstrings, reminding her of her warm child-hood home, so much so that she'd actually shiver and have to light a cigarette and contemplate her situation. Even the thought of an armchair would at times provide a sufficient and perfectly valid reason to make Jana feel sorry for herself. Because these were the exceptional moments when she still could be bothered with herself.

In the afternoon, Vivi was already in tears: about this not being the right moment for her to come, about how she shouldn't have come at all as she was trying to kick her habit. (But Jana had wanted her to come, anyway.) Just before Vivi burst into

tears they had sex, not very protracted and somehow hasty, seeing as they hadn't seen one another in such a long time. That's
why Jana claimed that she wanted it at least two more times
before dinner, insisting how much this sex meant to her and that
she'd derived more pleasure from it than anything else in a long
time, she insisted even when the third time around she practically masturbated while Vivi just held her with one arm and
kept wiping her own sweaty forehead with the other. Because
Vivi often simply wasn't *there*. She didn't have the energy for it.

After they'd had sex and Vivi had cried over herself and
bitched about her adverse life circumstances and finally fallen
asleep, Jana started dinner, still refusing to admit to herself the
relief she felt about having a couple of hours to herself. She
decided to make a pizza—you just throw some stuff on it and
pop it in the oven—she wasn't stoned enough to overreach herself and set about making trout amandine, for instance, or some
Melanesian dish. While cooking, she indulged in another form
of self-pity: positive daydreaming. Over-optimistic thoughts.
About how she and Vivi could be two happy, successful students
abroad. How everybody would say, oh, that's those two successful lesbians from the East, one's a humanities student, the other
one a physicist . . . And when they showed up at some women's
club they'd be a striking couple, like two ideal workers in a social
realist picture. Not that they'd actually look that way—only the
impression they'd create would be that strong. *Stronger than life
itself*—but this last sentence already pertained to the first rush of
her high; because while indulging in her upbeat thoughts Jana
had rolled an elegant slim joint for herself. As the pizza baked,
she sat and smoked, free to fantasize about how things might yet
turn out all right after all when Vivi had had the opportunity
to sleep off the long hours of the train journey. And it would
definitely be better in the evening when they went to the party
thrown by Jana's fellow students, whom they almost resembled
in age and appearance, almost . . . One of them a humanities
student, the other a mathematician, one dark-haired, the other

a redhead, no, one of them a brunette with red highlights, the other one with her head shaved. Oh, what difference does it make what color! The main thing is they'd embrace and gaze at the dark blue sky. She and Vivi.

"What are you looking at, honey?" Vivi asked.

"Nothing, what's there to look at?" grumbled Jana. She still had a slight advantage, being the one who'd wrapped gifts, cooked dinner and generally taken care of things while Vivi just nagged and napped, so for the time being Jana could still afford to be grumpy and even allow herself a snide remark—but soon Vivi would be so bitter and aggressive that Jana would fear for her (and months later, when she was alone, also for herself), which would make her act in a conciliatory fashion and not raise her voice at all. No, no, she's a far too responsible person for that. "Can I call home?" Vivi asked and lit a cigarette. As she put down the lighter she immediately noticed the lone butt of Jana's joint in the ashtray—she never missed things like that. "Yes, you may," said Jana. Then it occurred to her that before leaving they still had to eat and have a beer, and Vivi still had to shower and get dressed. And she wondered whether they'd last until the New Year, which was due to arrive at midnight that night.

At 8:20 p.m. they hurried along to catch the last train to Amsterdam. The last train to the New Year's Eve party. As a matter of fact, they dragged their feet because Vivi's legs hurt and she had to keep picking off the fine threads that had stuck to her face and body after she'd rubbed herself with one of Jana's old towels. Jana knew that Dutch trains didn't run after 8:00 p.m. on New Year's Eve, which made it abundantly clear just how pressed for time they were. So she told herself that what they were doing was hurrying along. Because if truth be told, Jana had failed to tell Vivi that there was probably no train left; she hadn't dared, because Vivi would've retorted: "Well, I guess I've screwed up again, haven't I?!" It would've been really dreadful if they'd missed the train and the New Year's Eve party in Amsterdam and Vivi blamed herself for that because she'd taken such a long time to shower and dress. When they hurried into the railroad station at 8:29, there was a single train standing at the platform—the 8:31 for Amsterdam. Thus they ended up sitting in a train, without even having bought a ticket, and Jana was in a considerably better frame of mind, despite Vivi's pathetic condition, because she knew how lucky they'd been to catch an unscheduled train. As the train rattled along, she stared through the window into the dark. Despite everything, it never occurred to her to get some new towels.

At 9:05 they were already in Amsterdam. When they stepped out into the main street leading to the Dam, Jana was suddenly overwhelmed by an inexplicable sense of anxiety, she wanted to go home, she wanted to go straight to Ljubljana, immediately, away from the wild looks, foreign languages, and whistling firecrackers. But she couldn't, so she asked her sweetheart: "Where shall we go? We've still got plenty of time." Vivi grimaced, halfway between tears and fury. Halfway. Jana was far too tired to listen, so she chose not to repeat the question. "Life sucks!" Vivi said to herself, though of course it was meant for the whole world to hear.

In what seemed like no time at all they'd reached the red light district. In no time at all. I could've avoided this, thought Jana, I could've taken her someplace else. But what would she actually have avoided? And where could they have gone, she and Vivi? It's all right the way it is, it was meant to be, said Jana to herself with a shadow of a smile. This was the third form of self-pity, this dogged resignation, this relentless and depressing surrender.

They marched in the cold, along a less crowded street in the vicinity of the red light district. "What do you mean, 'where shall we go.' How should I know?!" griped Vivi. Jana pretended not to be interested in the belated answer. They entered a crowded, smoke-filled, dimly lit bar and, surprisingly, found a free table in the small back room. Jana had a beer, her sweetheart didn't care what she had so Jana ordered a beer for her too. The silence, which had now lasted for several hours, was finally getting her down, but there was nothing she could talk about anyway. She could only find out something bad; she didn't want to hear anything about the things Vivi did during her absence, she didn't want to hear any lies along the lines of, "Just in case you happen to hear that I used to often go out with Teja, I'd better tell you myself that nothing happened between us." So she kept quiet, smoked and drank; she went to get herself another beer while Vivi had barely touched hers. Jana again lit up, drank, and stared emptily straight ahead. It was almost as quiet and gloomy as on the unscheduled train. Almost.

Then she saw him, an overweight fiftyish man sitting across from her. He'd sat down at their table so as to be very close to Vivi, who was practically squashed into the corner by his obesity. He smiled. Jana made a face, looked into her glass and downed the contents. But he'd smiled only at Vivi, stretching his upper lip so his unkempt black mustache bristled, revealing a plastic toothpick stuck between yellowing teeth. Vivi just looked at him. He proffered a hairy hand bedecked with thick gold rings, propelled the toothpick into a corner of his mouth, and addressed Vivi: *"My name is Hans."* He didn't introduce himself to Jana, who went for another beer at the same moment anyway. Jana disliked such assholes that invaded one's personal space and reminded her of the empty dimensions of the personal. But Vivi instantly transformed into a little girl, introduced herself, and looked at him like a little match girl starving on Christmas Eve. That's just it, thought Jana as she lit another cigarette, which already tasted disgustingly metallic, that's just it, Vivi was merely a little girl, lost and unprotected. Bah, Jana waved it off imperceptibly and thought: *Speak for yourself!* And this sudden insight into the little girl spiel was the second thing on that New Year's Eve to bring on a self-satisfied chuckle.

"Where are you from?" asked Hans. "Slovenia," said Vivi. Vivi enjoyed striking up acquaintances with strangers. "What about her?" he motioned toward Jana. "The same," said Vivi and smiled. *Man, I could punch you in the face*, thought Jana. "Where are you from?" asked Vivi. "Germany." Then a waitress came around and Hans asked Vivi what she'd like. She ordered a beer. Then she said to Jana: "Did you hear that, he says he's from Germany." Jana kept silent, it didn't seem worth it to start talking again just because of Hans, some Turk from Germany who happened to be sitting at their table.

Then Vivi said something Jana had never heard from her lips before, she said: "I'm sorry, I know you find him annoying." Hans didn't let that bother him at all. His mustache again spread above his smile, he reached out with his enormous paw and practically hugged Jana over the table. "Don't worry," he said. Then his face straightened and he looked at Vivi: "I know what you need."—"I don't know what you mean," she responded immediately. "Sure you do," said Hans, "and so does she." He wagged his head in Jana's direction. Vivi gave Jana a quick hug and said: "Leave her out of this." Jana drew back a little.

Hans put his tight fist on the tabletop in front of Vivi, then opened his shovel-like hand to reveal a neat little white packet. He wanted Vivi to give him her hand; he wanted her to place her palm into his. When Vivi reached out and surrendered her palm to his handshake, to quickly pocket the packet a few seconds later, Jana felt redundant. It made her think of elementary school, of the time in second grade when she snitched the memory-book of the boy who sat next to her in class. She didn't take it to keep it; she only wanted to draw something in it for him to remember her by—at that time she loved copying the graceful gazelle printed on the bag of a shoestore chain. The following day she returned the memory-book to her schoolmate. He gave her a surprised look and leafed through the book. Just as all the class rose to greet the teacher at the beginning of the lesson, her schoolmate showed her the picture she'd drawn and wagged a finger at her. Jana looked at him again—he was angry because he hadn't meant to give her his memory-book for her to write in at all. It made her ears burn in shame, and she felt so superfluous. And it was all her own fault.

When her ears burned, Jana knew it was a sign she'd gone too far.

They left the strange bar and Jana felt relieved, infinitely relieved. She fairly trembled with relief. Vivi was afraid Jana would demand to know what was in the small packet, and Jana was afraid Vivi would want to show her what was in the small packet. "You see the kind of things that happen to me? And there's nothing I can do about it, is there?" Vivi said. Fear is absolutely superfluous, thought Jana as she made a deprecating gesture; fear is no more than a habit. "You don't believe me, do you? Why don't you ever believe me? How am I supposed to change something if no one ever believes anything I say?" But Jana had been warding off change for a long time, because it was always for the worse. All that mumbo-jumbo about change being good got on her nerves—it must be good only for people who give advice and talk losers, who were incapable of lifting a finger to help themselves anyway, into changing.

Now they were walking along a relatively calm outlying part of the Red Light District, silently roving increasingly narrow streets that Jana wasn't very familiar with, but she was thinking about change anyway. And how good change was, once it was no longer necessary. If everything in life is all right, change is imperceptible, even unimportant, was her conclusion. And if . . .

"Hash, ecstasy!" two dealers behind a corner offered. Vivi pricked her ears and said: "No, thanks." Jana had been strolling along the streets of Amsterdam for weeks, she'd heard dealers' offers countless times, but she'd never heard anyone say to a dealer: *No, thanks.* When they reached the next corner, Jana stopped and said: "Wait, I don't know where we are." They stopped and Vivi immediately started feeling guilty, because she ostensibly felt too unwell to open the street map and look up street names. She felt too unwell to help herself, let alone anyone else. People always expected far too much from her anyway. Also Jana kept waiting for something all the time. It was true: Jana had been waiting for a long time indeed. Even abroad all she did was wait. She was sick and tired of waiting, so she arranged the oppressive days to structure her waiting; these were the only changes she introduced in her everyday life. To avoid major, more conspicuous changes. For that reason she'd go shopping every day or every second day, but without fail every Wednesday and Saturday.

"Speed and coke," they heard coming from behind their backs. Then a swarthy man in his thirties appeared before them. He wanted to know where they were from, he wanted to know what they were looking for; he said he had first-rate speed and coke at a reduced Christmas price. New Year's Eve stuff at a special New Year's Eve price. Vivi said they were from Slovenia and no, thank you, they weren't looking for anything, they'd just lost their way.

"What about you? Are you looking for something?" Speed-and-Coke asked Jana. "No, thanks," she said. Then she asked him where he was from, because she somehow felt she had to make conversation. Speed-and-Coke said he was Italian, or not exactly Italian, but close, and that he'd been to beautiful Slovenia once. "What did you do in Slovenia?" Vivi asked him. "I've got other stuff as well," he said and lowered his voice con-spiratorially. Jana gestured to Vivi and they set off toward the Dam, or at least they thought that was the direction they took. "Hey, girls," he called after them, "it's New Year's Eve, relax! I've got other stuff as well. Trip is on sale too, if you know what I mean."

And if . . . things aren't that all right, then change is just so much more shit, decided Jana, and abandoned her self-pitying contemplation. She sat down on the curb and immersed her-self in the city map. When she happily announced she'd found the way to the party at her friends' place, Vivi said her legs were really killing her. So really killing her she simply had to rest a bit. Or maybe grab a beer in a bar. When Jana resigned herself to the fact that they'd have to take a taxi to her friends' place, Vivi sat down next to her on the curb and puckered her face; she was about to start crying. Had Jana looked at her, Vivi would've burst into tears. That's why Jana kept her eyes riveted on the map. "You know . . . ," Vivi said uncertainly. "What?" said Jana, and lit a cigarette. Also Vivi lit one and said: "Honey, there's something I've got to tell you." Not now, thought Jana, not now of all times, I don't want any more changes at least until the New Year. Vivi's face contorted again, this time because she couldn't bring herself to utter the words. Who the hell was it? Jana wondered. Teja? Urša? Leja? A moment later her ears began to burn. "You know . . ." Vivi started again and crushed her cigarette under her foot. "You know . . . well, I'm trying to kick my habit."

Jana folded the city map and got to her feet. She readjusted her woolen hat, wrapped the scarf tighter around her neck, and shoved her hands deep into the shallow pockets. Then she repeated the whole procedure two more times. Every time she wrapped the scarf tighter around her neck. "What are you doing? You want me to bring you a beer from a bar too?" Vivi asked. "Nothing, I'm just showing the symptoms," Jana laughed. "Yeah, bring me a Foster's. In a can—please."

An hour or two later they stood in a phone booth and laughed. Jana called her friends to tell them she and Vivi wouldn't be coming over, that they'd wait for the New Year on the Dam and that they could all get together later in a club. "Have we solved all the problems now?" Vivi asked playfully. "Every single one of them. We no longer have to look at this stupid map," answered Jana and smiled. "Really, truly?" asked Vivi. "And we haven't spoiled our New Year's Eve?" Jana embraced her and crushed the can in her hand. Vivi hugged her tight and whispered quietly: "Shall we go to the Dam now? Aren't we going to miss the New Year?" Jana re-wrapped her scarf around her neck: "You know that can't happen . . . it's impossible for anyone to be late for the New Year."

And they weren't, either. They were never late for a train again, or anything else, ever.

TRANSLATED BY TAMARA SOBAN

DISCRETION GUARANTEED

The beaten path I set out on swept through meadows, and in the distance wriggled its way into a condensed handful of village houses. That's where I was supposed to turn left. Or so I was told by the friend who dropped me off not far from the highway access ramp. As he drove on, I continued to look back at his blue Renault 4. I wondered whether he'd still see me were I to wave to him, and if so, would he stop and wait for me if I changed my mind. I convinced myself that it was too late and forced myself to move on, downward, along the path, through the meadows. *After you turn left, you'll surely meet someone who'll direct you to the Korošak house,* the letter said. *If there's no one around, just go straight on a little more and cross the stream and our house is right there.* I'd already read her letter several times. Even so, walking on that path between those meadows, I pulled it out of my pocket and tried to make out more from it than had actually been written. I noted again the style of writing and the grammatical errors, the small slanted letters that reminded me of those in a primary school reader—properly formed, inexpressive.

Nearby, a little bridge crossed the dried out stream. To hide from possible glances from houses on the other side, I stood behind a tree. I read the poster nailed to the trunk—in a neighboring village a well-known Croatian singer would be performing at an upcoming festival—and then I looked at her letter to check the house number, as though I hadn't memorized it two weeks ago when I first read it.

Finally I stepped away from the tree trunk, crossed the bridge and approached the house. I rang the doorbell and stood waiting. I began to feel that I'd made a mistake, that I'd taken a wrong step, that I'd landed in some different but parallel universe. I took no comfort in knowing that I'd come to the correct village and the correct address in that village. When she finally opened the door, she looked at me with an expression of surprise, and I was certain she had no idea who I was. Then it seemed as though something slipped over her face and she relaxed. We shook hands.

"Oh well, sorry, I completely forgot about the time—two, right? I'm Manja."

This was Manja from the photo. I recognized the beauty mark above her left eyebrow and her full lips, but in person she had a much softer facial expression. After we shook hands she didn't release mine and for a moment we stood looking at each other. Then, perhaps realizing that it wasn't smart to remain on the doormat, she led me inside. I considered asking her that polite question about taking my shoes off, but a first look at the unfurnished house told me it wasn't necessary.

"We haven't finished the house yet. And there won't be enough money this year either . . ."

I asked myself what she meant by *we*, whom did she number herself among. Wasn't it out of the ordinary and extremely pretentious to refer to oneself in the plural?

"Please." She showed me the stairs that were still without a banister. "Go right on up, there's only one room. I mean, there are, rather there will be more rooms, but there aren't any doors yet. Should I get some coffee?"

I nodded and went upstairs, leaning against the blood-red bricks of the unplastered wall. Among the mess of clothes and children's toys, I found a low leather armchair covered with shirts and bibs. I threw them on the floor and sat down. The room, which was obviously the only one in the house being used for dwelling, wasn't any less messy. The only thing that indicated even a modicum of stability was a giant cabinet, placed in the center of the room. Behind it, the rest of the belongings were packed in enormous bags and cardboard boxes. Through the cabinet's glass, I saw tea and coffee sets and porcelain figurines of ballerinas, with the faces of small gnomes and soldiers scattered among them. On the right side were books that had been placed with care: among them volumes from the Hundred Novels collection, and even more from the series of the adventures of the French heroine, Marianne.

"Careful, it's hot!" could be heard from the foot of the stairs. "Stay downstairs in the kitchen!"

Manja brought a large tray of coffee, sugar, and milk. When she placed it on the table, she said: "There, now."

I began to feel that I was stuck in a predicament. Without hesitating, I took the cup of coffee, added a bit of milk, and began sipping while it was still hot. At the same time, I looked around the room so that my eyes wouldn't have to meet hers.

"I know, the place is a mess," said Manja. "I haven't gotten around to it yet. It's only been a few months since we moved in. Since I had to find work, I haven't had time for tidying up."

I nodded. I didn't know what to say. Maybe the whole thing would turn out to be a mistake now. A woman who says things like that couldn't have possibly written the ad I read. In which case, I was drinking the wrong coffee and getting involved in the wrong conversation. I tried to think of something polite to ask her. But her eyes were already focused on something else.

"Didn't I tell you two to stay downstairs?"

When I turned around I saw two children standing right behind me, a girl about four years old with a dirty face, and a boy with a runny nose who appeared a year or two younger. I smiled at them and then, embarrassed, I once again turned to the hostess. I never had the slightest clue how to act with kids.

"Now that there are two of them, it's even worse," said Manja. "What I'm saying is that no one listens at all anymore." At the repeated request to go down to the kitchen, they discreetly crept away.

"I really love reading your letters," she suddenly changed

the subject as though realizing that our time was limited, that the last bus out of this village would be leaving in only a few short hours.

"Yeah, well it was a pleasure writing them," I reply without thinking. A yin should have its yang, after all.

"No one's visited me till now," Manja lights a cigarette and blows the smoke loudly. She offers me one. "Till now, not one of the women who answered my ad has come to visit me. And I haven't visited anyone. Nobody."

"Why not?" I ask, though it's clear that the answer to this question is of absolutely no importance to either of us.

"I don't know. I don't have time. Sometimes I lack the courage. To be honest, I'm never actually at home by myself."

As I listen, I try to place her spoken words next to the ones that she'd written. *I know what I am. It's all I desire to be. It's still not too late.* Confirming her identity was obviously of great importance to her. *Only once, well, twice if I count the time with the foreign woman on the high school graduation trip, I slept with a woman. It wasn't by chance. It wasn't something I could forget.*

"You have to take your time," I say and for the first time in my life, it's clear to me that this expression didn't start out as a cliché. Though I can't know for sure because I wasn't there when it started out.

"You know that I'm married, don't you?" When her spoken words overlap with those of her letters, we're suddenly totally distant. It was easier communicating with her through words on a page than face-to-face. Our proximity seemed to eclipse the understanding we'd built through our letters, and her physical presence came at me like a shout.

"Where's your husband?" I reluctantly ask her.

"Mostly traveling. On a ship. His job."

When she reaches for a cigarette, I get the feeling that she wants to touch me. My hand is hidden under the table; hers grasps a full ashtray, which she takes to the bin next to the window.

"Oh, OK," I say to her back.

I now regret that she didn't touch me. We're running out of time. There's probably only one bus that leaves this village per day.

"I mean, a person can be lonely here . . . ," she says, sitting back down and moving her chair closer to me. "If she's *like this*."

I shrug. "You can get lonely in the city too. I mean, I'm lonely too. In the city. Well, not always." I let out a cough; speaking these words has suddenly become a terrible burden.

"Really? But I don't even have anyone to talk to." Manja lowered her head as though in shame, as though she'd opened up to a stranger for nothing. I took her hand, because I felt I owed her something. Her slender hand was cold and stiff with fear and expectations. She reached for me with her other hand as though she was going to hug me, but her forearm brushed against my neck for only a second. Then I let go, I somehow shook off her damp palms.

"There probably isn't a bus now," is what I impersonally said. I was afraid to give her anything, even if only false promises and expectations.

I'm terrified of lesbians who live in hiding, who live in the shadow of their husbands and their loving children, women who exist among books inherited from family, books stacked behind glass and bearing titles like *Kristin Lavransdatter* and *White Tulips* and *Your Married Life Together*. I'm terrified of these women who live in half-completed houses, their memories of naked women's bodies hidden in the dark, their longings suppressed.

I put out my cigarette and stood up. Manja stood up too, quickly, spilled her coffee, stepped toward me and grabbed me by the elbows.

"You know why no one's come to visit me yet? Why I still haven't met even one of those women yet?" she asked.

"I don't know. Why?"

"Because not one of them wrote letters like yours. I read

your letters incessantly." I kissed her. She was different from the others, I said to myself. In the key moment, she didn't complain about her loneliness. She didn't swear by eternity and harmony. She didn't beg, she took. She didn't return only the kiss to me. She returned everything.

The bus left ten minutes before schedule, typical of village buses. Good thing I'd arrived a half hour early. I'm glad that she didn't accompany me. She was also relieved that she didn't have to walk with me and be in sight of eyes peering from the neighboring houses. I think this was the right way to do it. That everything was okay. The longings satisfied, the loneliness elim-inated once again, if only for a moment. Neither of us wanted more than that anyhow, I say to myself. At least not at that same address. There's no need for me to remember the number of the house. Nor to write her again. Over and over, I try to avoid them, these hidden sapphists in disguise.

Friend of Sappho, twenty-four years old, lonely, attached, seeks similar, a woman whose soul feels the same, for conversation, shar-ing most secret thoughts, and possible romantic encounter. Should be between twenty-five and thirty-five years old, sincere, independent and understanding. Alcoholics and players need not apply. Write today: discretion guaranteed.

TRANSLATED BY ELIZABETA ŽARGI, REVISED BY BETH ADLER

LETTERS WITHOUT ENVELOPES

Mara's first letter came in the autumn of the late 1980s. The fact that she'd gotten my address in Switzerland, as she explained at the beginning, seemed incredible to me, almost mysterious. She lived in Dalmatia, in a town I'd never been to. She wrote me a two-page letter, mentioning more than once that she was a lesbian, probably the only one in Dalmatia, if not the whole of Croatia. For a number of years, she'd been visiting her uncle in Zürich and particularly her friend Uli, whom she'd met at the city's lesbian center. Uli was therefore the only lesbian she knew. But on her last visit to Zürich, her Swiss friend had assured her that she was no longer the only lesbian in Yugoslavia. There was at least one other in the country who'd been to several international conferences. The lesbian center archive had received a report from a conference, along with the list of names and addresses of the participants. And so Uli found the address of another Yugoslav lesbian and passed it on to Mara.

She replied to my first letter on seven full pages. At first, she didn't believe I even existed, so she decided to wait with her life story. Seeing as I participated in international lesbian meetings, she also assumed that I surely must have moved to some Western European country by then. She didn't know much about what was happening in Ljubljana; the lesbian and gay movement was barely mentioned in the Croatian press. So I sent her some information about our groups and the lesbian bulletin. I wanted to be as supportive as I could to my new Dalmatian friend; the nineties were approaching of course, the time when words and phrases embodying whole concepts began to enter general usage:

empowerment, gay affirmative therapy, awareness groups, silence equals death, fight against social isolation, lesbian ghetto . . . Mara responded by describing her isolated, private fate. More than anything, she wished for a lover, a true partner, but in her environment, that was virtually impossible. Even talking about it was barely acceptable for reasons of personal safety. She'd sent a personal ad to some Croatian magazine, writing that she wanted to meet an intimate friend "who wasn't a stranger to love between women." A couple of days later, she received a kind letter from the editor saying that she completely understood and supported her in her quest for love, but that, unfortunately, such an ad could not be published in the lonely hearts column, as the editorial policy didn't allow the advertisement of questionable sexual practices, which, unfortunately, also included lesbian love. And so, in addition to her kind rejection, she also sent her back the money for the ad.

It was clear to me that there wasn't much I could do for Mara in that respect. So I simply invited her to come to the lesbian film festival in Ljubljana, telling her that she could stay with me in my rented room, if she didn't have a problem with that.

Her reply came after nearly two months, which was a little unusual, given our regular correspondence in the past. She was excited and wrote that she was in love with her coworker. Happily in love! That the impossible had happened: she'd invited her for dinner and, over a nice fish and a bottle of wine on the table, she took a chance and confessed her love for her. Her coworker Ana was very understanding, she even said that she really liked Mara too, but had never considered that there could be anything more to it. And after a couple of weeks of constant companionship, their friendship had grown into something more. Much more, in fact.

In December, when the week of the film festival began, Mara did come to Ljubljana, even though her Ana couldn't take time off from work. I was slightly nervous as I waited for her at the train station, the way I'd sometimes been uneasy and

anxious before when I was about to meet someone I knew very
well through letters, knowing that no matter what, a complete
stranger would soon be standing before me in person. As soon
as Mara got off the Split-Ljubljana train, I knew it was she,
although she was completely different of course than I'd imagined her based on our correspondence. She had shoulder-length
dark hair, a brown suede jacket, Levi's jeans, and sneakers. All
that she brought with her was a medium-sized bag with a single
strap over her bony shoulder. She smiled at me briefly when she
saw me, and held out her hand. After exchanging a few short
questions and answers as we were leaving the station, it was clear
to me that she was the reserved and quiet type. That was what I
was most afraid of. I'd never been good at taking initiative in a
casual chat. And so, by the time we were on the bus on our way
to my apartment, we were already more or less silent.

We didn't talk much in the next couple of days either. In
the evenings, we went to film screenings, and during the day
we tried to stay out of each other's way as much as possible.
If I made us lunch, she didn't have any special demands, she
was happy with whatever was on the table. Otherwise, she only
drank water and didn't smoke. She wasn't even bothered by the
fact that there was no radiator in the bathroom; she told me that
she was used to unheated spaces from home. Apparently, out of
some conviction that the cold could never be that bad in their
parts, Dalmatians didn't have heating at all in the wintertime.

On the last day of the festival they were showing the German
film *November Moon* about two women in love during the Third
Reich. The woman who'd been hiding her Jewish lover in her
apartment all through the war and even applied for an admin-
istrative position in the Nazi propaganda department in order
to avoid any house searches by the Gestapo and was generally
trying to be as inconspicuous as possible, was accused of collab-
orating with the Nazis after the war. A group of women grabbed
her on the street and punished her by shaving her head. Her
Jewish friend, who dared to go out into the free streets for the

very first time, found her lying on the pavement in the middle of the city, beaten, disgraced, with a crazy look in her eyes that didn't bode well.

In the evening, I offered Mara a glass of wine, although she'd been strictly ascetic until then. She accepted.

"I can't get that film out of my mind," she said, staring at a corner of the room. "How high the price you have to pay for love is sometimes, don't you think?"

I shrugged. I guessed so, but at that point, I didn't have to pay anything, I was happily single.

"In times of war, many people pay dearly if they truly love someone," I said after a while. "True," said Mara, and unexpectedly gestured toward my pack of cigarettes.

I nodded in surprise as she lit herself a cigarette, casually inhaling and exhaling smoke like an experienced smoker.

"This is an exception," she said, holding up her cigarette. "I light up sometimes. I also lit myself one when I was coming on to Ana. What was it I wanted to say again?"

"Actually, I said that in times of war, love costs everyone dearly," I said.

"But we're in war all the time, *kužiš*—get it?"

She started telling me the story about her quest for love. When that magazine had rejected her ad, she completely gave up for a while. She started thinking of moving to her uncle's in Zürich, where she at least knew Uli. She was bound to meet a lot of friends through the lesbian scene there sooner or later. But one night, she was lying in bed, unable to go to sleep, not knowing what she was to do. Should she even persist and go on living this miserable existence? She couldn't remember why she eventually started thinking about how many literary protagonists had sold their soul to the devil for various earthly pleasures. She couldn't think of a single woman protagonist who'd done something like that. She was toying with a fantastic idea that she could be the woman who'd sell her soul to the devil—in exchange for a lover. Only she didn't know how to go about it; how on earth did a lonely and desperate soul get in contact with Satan himself? With that question in mind, she finally fell asleep. When she woke up the following morning, her head hurt and she thought that she'd heard thunder in her sleep.

"But that can't mean anything," I said carefully, as if kindly reminding her that superstition, after all, was without any real foundation, as she surely must have known.

"I know, I know," she said distantly, still absorbed in the story. A few days later, her eyes fell on her coworker Ana. All of a sudden, it seemed to her that she was different, more open and understanding than others. Not only smart, but also subtle and attractive, though inconspicuous. Then she thought that Ana was indeed special. So very special that she not only fell in love with her, but also dared to believe that she could return her love. Or would at least know how to keep quiet if she turned her down. And she'd almost certainly turn her down because she wasn't a lesbian. Eventually, Mara took a chance and asked her out to dinner. She swore to herself that she'd try this direct and risky move and if she failed, she'd have a strong reason for seriously considering moving to Zürich.

"You know the rest," Mara said.

I nodded.

"I can't believe I met such an interesting girl as my Ana. That we love each other . . . I only hope that we'll leave some day, before we suffocate in Dalmatia. We have a problem neither of us had known before: constant and systematic hiding."

Naturally no one knew the true nature of their relationship. Not their parents, nor their friends, least of all their coworkers. Mara knew what her family thought of homosexual scum, she knew too well how her sisters would sometimes make fun of the foreign faggots who were beaten up when the locals tracked them down on some beach and how their father would spit out of the window with disgust hearing their tales. All of a sudden, Mara and Ana started behaving very cautiously toward their relatives, like thieves who knew that the only hope they had, besides of course luck, was not being caught stealing, otherwise they'd have their fingers chopped off.

"Well, things aren't that much better here," I said.

"But . . ." Mara had no need for my comments. "And children are the worst. Ana and I often go for a walk because we can't be alone anywhere, unless my family or hers aren't home. We walk along the beach, find some secluded spot, sit on the rocks and talk. We never touch in public. It's happened more than once that a bunch of elementary school kids turned up and I had no idea at first why they were fixated on the two of us, what was so interesting to them about two grown women sitting and talking. Ana once said to me in horror: 'Children know!' They have no reserve and scream out loud that we're dykes or start giggling, asking which one of us is the man and if we shared a dick between us. They say all the things that our colleagues at work would never dare say out loud, though some of them probably think something even worse, and that our families prefer not to be aware of."

"You'll leave one day," I said.

"That's what keeps me going. But there's something else."

I was afraid there was something wrong between them as well.

"No, no, we love each other very much!" she assured me. "But I get scared sometimes when I dream about this weird man that's haunting me. I dream that I'm walking down the street, I'm usually late for work, and all of a sudden, I find myself on the outskirts of the town, all alone. In one instant, I'm on my guard, I think that something creepy is going on. There's some-thing ominous in the air. Something sticky. Although I'm out in the open, I feel completely enclosed, confined. I turn around and suddenly an old man is standing behind me with a bike. He only watches me from under the cap hiding his eyes. But I feel it on my skin that his gaze is burning like coal."

"And what happens then?" I ask anxiously. I myself am a bit frightened, but that makes the story all the more interesting.

"Nothing." Mara shrugs. "I see him in my dreams over and over again, suddenly standing behind me, or just feel that he's somewhere outside my field of vision, like the bogeyman from American horror movies. And then I wake up. Here's what scares me the most: that the devil's going to take my woman away the same way he gave her to me."

I'm almost certain that I've dreamed about this man or at least imagined him. "Does he have anything with him?" I ask Mara.

"Yes, that's right! He has an old wicker basket on the handlebar of his bike, the kind women at the market use to carry their fruit in . . ."

"But there's no fruit in it . . ." I add.

"I never see its content. And plastic bags hang from the other side of the handlebar. There's something slimy in them, dark, it looks like big chunks of spoiled meat or a coiled-up snake."

We finally stop scaring each other with horror stories and go to bed.

"I'm not surprised you find the old man with the bike familiar," says Mara after I turn off the light. "Ana also thinks she's seen him before, in her dreams, in films or just her imagination . . ."

"The Dark Man . . ." I mumble.

"What did you say?"

"In Slovenia, we call him the Dark Man."

The following summer, I visited Mara and Ana in Dalmatia. The two of them were supposed to come to Ljubljana soon, but then I moved and they both had jobs, as well as increased workloads at the university, so we kept putting off seeing each other.

And then I saw the news showing the footage of the Yugoslav army bombing cities in south Dalmatia. One of the places was where my friends lived. I didn't hear from either of them for a long time and then, one day, another letter from Mara finally came from the town under siege. She was alone, for her beloved had to leave Dalmatia with her Serbian family. They moved to

southern Serbia. Ana was stuck in an unfamiliar Serbian city
that she'd never been to before, while Mara was stuck in her
Dalmatian hometown that was under constant attack. As the
postal service between Croatia and Serbia was suspended, Mara
asked me if I could send her letters for Ana to Serbia and Ana
would send me her letters for Mara, which I would then send to
Dalmatia. I was their courier for several years. Eventually, they
no longer wrote much to me, the envelopes contained only their
letters for each other, and to me they would sometimes write:
"Thank you!" It seemed a small miracle to me that the postal
service functioned at all during the war. So that Mara, sitting
by the candlelight in the basement, where all of her family had
moved, could write long letters to her beloved, put them in
an envelope and send them to me. I couldn't imagine how she
even managed to post them, where she got the stamps, whether
she took the letter to the post office or just put it in the nearest
post box, if she could leave the house at all, if anyone actually
emptied the post boxes, if there even was an intact post box to
be found in the city under constant siege.

Mara's letters for Ana were sent open; she didn't put them in
a separate envelope. Sometimes, when I was stuffing the numer-
ous pages of her tiny handwriting into an envelope with Ana's
Serbian address, my eyes would steal a glance at a sentence or
two. I'd rather not know how much she missed her. Sometimes,
she'd also make a drawing of her and Mara embracing or kissing.
Under one of these drawings, I read that she'd go crazy if she
couldn't touch Ana soon. And in one of the following letters,
she did write to me that she'd set out on a long, incredible,
and dangerous journey from the besieged town to the north of
Croatia and then across Hungary to southern Serbia. She'd spent
a few days with Ana, where her dreams of moving in with Ana's
Serbian relatives as a Croatian national were shattered. She'd
never be able to get a job, just like there was almost no chance of
Ana ever getting Croatian citizenship after her father had been
deported for working for the Yugoslav navy. Once again, they

were trying to come up with new ways and plans to be together, this time for real, perhaps even in Slovenia or still further north or west, as far away as possible from this bloodshed.

In the mid-nineties, an East European lesbian and gay conference was organized in Ljubljana. Unexpectedly, Mara and Ana were there as well. They'd been living abroad for a number of years then, first in Zürich, then Amsterdam, before eventually settling in London. They were finally able to rent an apartment together, go to work in the same city again, buy themselves a car, put potted plants on the balcony in the summer, take the dog to the vet for its shot, then finally end their long relationship, break up, remain close friends and come to the conference, each with her new girlfriend—things that are only possible when living in peace, without hiding in the basement. We talked about activism in Slovenia, Croatia, England, about new political issues, the spread of intolerance in Europe, the decline of the classic forms of feminism, the breakthrough of Slovenian psychoanalysis and the illusions of the Internet revolution. We mentioned neither the past war nor the letters that had made us allies without words.

Ever since we've become so dependent on e-mail, Mara and I only rarely exchange a short message or two. This and this is happening here, are you coming, what's new, how's life. I'm simply unable to write such letters on the computer as I used to write on paper that responds, and produces a scraping sound under the pen, until you finally fold the letter, put it in an envelope, stick on the stamp if you have it at home, or take it to the post office.

It was letters I was thinking of when I chanced upon an American documentary on the television about the recent war in Croatia. It also featured edited footage from Mara's besieged town. I turned up the volume. Amid the noise of falling bombs and a few rare running civilians and armed soldiers on the streets, I saw a familiar figure in the background. There he stood, by his bike, his face half-hidden under his ragged cap. His eyes couldn't be seen. He stood there, calmly watching the mayhem in the street from the background. The Dark Man. Then he raised his head slightly and I could feel his burning eyes; he threw something away behind his back, quickly rummaged through the dirty bags hanging from the handlebar—the old wicker basket was no longer to be seen—and swayed away from the scene on his bike. On the spot where he'd stood, a yellow post box was revealed.

TRANSLATED BY ŠPELA BIBIČ

THE GREENHOUSE

It's dark in the kitchen, too dark to see all the tacky new furniture. Ana's father heaps generous helpings of potatoes and salad onto his plate, which is already overflowing with pieces of meat. "My old man eats like a pig," she told me not long after we met and started sharing our personal histories.

I met Ana when she was carrying dirt. Well, not dirt but bags of black soil for planting. This was sometime in the last, cold autumn when I really needed the money, so I took a two-week student job working at a new garden center called Lustig Leben, crammed in between the complexes of the new industrial zone. It was a nine- to ten-hour job but you got a hot lunch (with a vegan option) and 850 tolars an hour. First I had to carry light wooden crates with plants to greenhouse number three while Ana carried the bags of dirt, and then we did the planting together. The first time I saw her, she was wearing a red checkered shirt, a bag slung over her shoulder. After she walked into the greenhouse and threw the bag down on the ground with a deep sigh, she immediately held out her right hand to introduce herself, holding two cans of beer in her left. I wondered many times why she brought two of them; how she knew I was there. But I never asked her that. "I'm always thirsty here," she said. "I'm Ana, by the way. My real name is Anamarija, but I don't like to be called that. You're new, aren't you? Student job?" She also told me that her old man was really into gardening so she knew quite a lot about it herself, and that she was taking some business classes, but they weren't really her thing. She didn't like gardening either. She preferred to do fieldwork—counting traffic and such.

I liked Ana right away. Maybe because I'd never seen her around before and because it's always a big deal to meet someone new and interesting in this small town. And Ana was one of those rare people who like their beer with foam. She always poured it into a glass and then dove into the foam with her mouth. "Beer without a head on it is no beer at all," she'd say. And that always made me think she must do the same thing when she dove into a woman's crotch. I think what made me like going to work at the greenhouse so much were the conversations with Ana as we bent over some seedlings, the fact that we always made sure there was beer, and that we smoked pot hiding behind some cypress trees in glazed pots. Ana was often thirsty; in fact she was thirsty all the time. After work we'd go for a beer, saying we deserved a nice peaceful drink sitting down. Then we told each other everything about our childhoods. About school and friends. Ana talked about her sporting achievements in high school, about junior varsity and national teams and all those terms I didn't understand because I hated sports in high school. I listened to her patiently, nodding in agreement at her explanation as to why she eventually gave up competitive sports. But I thought to myself that those were actually the only achievements in her life.

When we got high together for the first time in her rented basement room, she told me she didn't want to live at home because her folks got on her nerves. "I have nothing against them, they just drive me crazy. They always want something from me. I wouldn't mind getting something from them, too, but I know there's no point—they just weren't meant to be parents. Sometimes I go have Sunday dinner with them, but even that's a pain. My mom fiddles around with the pots and pans and the vacuum cleaner like she wants me to help her or something, and dad's always out in the garden tending his flowers and lettuce. But I don't lift a finger. I can't wait for the dinner to be over, for Dad to polish off those endless potatoes and meat, and for Mom to throw the plates in the sink and then I'm out of there."

But that really wasn't news to me.

So I really have no idea what I'm doing at a family dinner at her parents' house. The soup noodles are slightly undercooked, the potatoes are too greasy, I don't eat meat and I'd rather not have the salad because I'm afraid it has worms in it. All I can think about is when are we going to get out of here. Why do we even have to be here. "Don't worry about them. Just eat your food and to hell with them," Ana says. I really don't give a damn how her old man is. Her mother is trying to be nice but I find her efforts a bit annoying. Her husband does too, which is why he keeps throwing irritated looks her way. Finally her mom stops trying and sits down. A faint smile flickers across her face with each scoop of the ladle. Her old man slurps his soup. I look at them and wonder how they could've had a daughter like Ana. Ana's at least half a head taller than either of them. I don't know what I liked about her more: the blonde hair cascading down the nape of her neck, or her red-checked shirt. But I'm not keen on everything that surrounds her. I don't care about her fieldwork, I'm not interested in her friends, or her brothers and sisters, much less in her accomplishments as an athlete in grade school. I've come to realize I don't like anything of hers, anything that places her here in this city. The only thing I can stand about her is her and I want her to remain my discovery, somebody none of my Ljubljana friends know. So I prefer to see her at my place, away from her life, which I would rather strip off her. I do go to her place and sometimes I feel very close to her, like today at this family dinner, but somehow I'm not at the right party, as if I'm at a concert listening to my Walkman.

Around the time I stopped working at Lustig Leben garden center and my barhopping, beer-drinking period came to an end, Ana went to visit her sister in Germany. When she came back, I couldn't readjust to her, as if I'd already forgotten her.

I still had her phone number on a piece of paper and hadn't yet added it to my address book. That's what I do with the phone numbers and the addresses of people I know I'll only need once and never again or when one of my friends happens to be staying with them. So things weren't going as smoothly as they did before; it's as if we were only meant to be planting, drinking and smoking buddies in that greenhouse. Both of us had changed. Ana talked about other things, for instance, that she was thinking of going back to school. I hardly talked about anything anymore. Not even about myself, much less about her plans for self-betterment. Sometimes I didn't pick up the phone because I didn't know what to say to her. Because I had neither the time nor the desire to go out for a beer. But sometimes she'd show up drunk and stoned on my doorstep after midnight— that's when she wanted me most—and I thought it was good to know Ana, after all.

But in the morning I thought how good it was to have a job again, because that meant Ana would be leaving after the first cup of coffee. And I didn't need to feel bad anymore. Maybe I've lost that hick trait they call character.

On my way to work—actually I don't have a regular job, I'm an eternal part-timer; but sometimes it's a relief to be able to say you're going to work, and that way nobody asks, well, what about insurance, don't you realize what hard times these are—at any rate, on my way to work, outside this little café, I ran into Samir. I couldn't turn him down when he invited me to join him for a cup of coffee. Not him, of all people. We'd met seven years ago when the war in Yugoslavia broke out. He deserted from the army, fled Bosnia, and came to live with his sister in Ljubljana. He'd heard about the gay scene here and came to the office on Kersnik Street. The war was spreading like wildfire all the way to Croatia, while Samir and I sat in that stuffy office on a summer afternoon—at that point, I had a full-time job as a trainee—talking about how the gay movement in the former

Yugoslavia hadn't been going anywhere, anyway. Then he borrowed some foreign gay magazines and some porn on cassette. "I'll stop by tomorrow," he said each time.

"I have my own business now," he told me as we sat outside the café. "It's not going as well as it should, but I get by. You know, I'd like to help out a friend . . ."

He told me his life story, which was sad, of course. What else is new, I thought. What else is new, besides a young man from a poor rural family who has a rich older "friend," who, in his heart, really wants to be in Ljubljana with Samir. "It's a good thing that you're going to try to help him if he comes here on account of you," I thought out loud. "Of course I will," Samir said enthusiastically. "I always help. You helped me when I came to Ljubljana seven years ago and didn't know a living soul. I always help, but I don't let people take advantage of me." Again I agreed. I've been agreeing with people a lot lately. Even with my late grandmother, who read *The Orphan of Lowood* or *Jane Eyre* six times and regularly went to the movies in the summer to cry watching *One Day of Life*, but otherwise nothing was free, according to her. "You know, Suzana, in life it's always like this: whatever you get, you're going to have to give back sooner or later, but whatever you give is gone for good," she told me gently once when I turned up my nose at her because she wouldn't let the little girl who lived next door use our toilet. I looked at her in amazement and suddenly, in the face of her profound wisdom, I felt ashamed. I wiped away my tears. "There, there," said Grandma. "You know, it costs money to have the cesspool cleaned."

A lot had happened to Samir in the seven years we hadn't seen each other. He was disappointed, of course. He only did clean deals now—in business and in love. He'd figure something out with this boy, too, or else leave him in the countryside with his sugar daddy. He just wasn't financially successful enough or anywhere near old enough, for that matter, to be supporting other people. "I'm twenty-five," he said proudly. "I'm going to give this serious relationship stuff one more go, and then I'm done." Again I agreed, then finished my coffee and went on my way.

"Why won't you give it a chance?" Ana asked me not long after my first—and hopefully last—dinner with her parents.

"Give what a chance?" I asked.

"Us. You know, why won't you give us a chance?"

We're not alike. But we're not so different, either. There are certain things we can't talk about. She doesn't know my all-time favorite movies and she doesn't appreciate the music that pumps me up. And I don't care what it's like to do fieldwork and count traffic. The only thing I can still do is agree. To be perfectly honest, it's not that simple and the differences between us aren't as clear as I'd like them to be. Frankly, my list of the greatest films of all time hasn't changed for at least ten years and I only rarely go to the movies anymore. And when Ana isn't counting traffic, she reads books. Still, there are certain things we can't talk about. Even if it's only because I don't feel like it anymore. Ana has plans. After good sex Ana always has plans for the future and an interest in taking classes. But I have no interest in encouraging her—I don't betray those principles anymore.

"You know, I bumped into a friend from Bosnia the other day. He lives in Ljubljana now."

I didn't answer her question.

"And?"

"Nothing. I can't forget what he said about giving steady relationships one more go and then he's done."

"And? What are you trying to say?"

"Nothing. I'm just thinking. I'm trying to think when the last time was. We never know, do we?"

But it always costs money to have the cesspool cleaned. I felt sorry for the little girl next door. A hundred years ago when I was little and she was even littler, she had to pee so badly that she cut through yards holding her hand between her legs to keep from having an accident as she ran home to the toilet. Maybe there's some other way, I thought desperately, but I didn't have the guts to say that to Grandma. When the time comes to have the cesspool cleaned, you just send everyone who's been using your toilet a note or a bill. Like when it came time to butcher the animals. When we butchered a pig, we shared the meat, the blood sausages, and the baked blood with all of our neighbors. And all the neighbors would do the same; butchering time was always an event for the whole block, not just one family. But I guess that was only because there were no freezers back then.

But I didn't say anything.

Because my grandmother had told me of the dreadful fate of the orphan of Lowood so many times. "That's suffering you can't even imagine. You have no idea how good you have it." And I felt ashamed.

"So you're not going to give us a chance, not really."

"I didn't say that."

"Yes, you did. You said you didn't know when the last time was—for you."

"I do know."

We were silent. What was I supposed to say?

"It annoys me that you don't like me," Ana went on. "And that you won't tell me you don't."

That's not true at all. There are so many things I like about her. Everything—her hair, her eyes, her body, even the smell of her sweaty skin. Her exasperation at not being able to win me over completely. Her frustration and rage at not being born to smarter parents who'd have forced her to go to school, forbidden her to smoke pot at sixteen and hang out with bad guys. When she finished venting her anger at her family and the world and the unfairness of it all, she started breathing deeply, threw off her shirt and said, "Oh, to hell with everything . . . everything" at least two times before reaching her hand under my T-shirt.

"That's right . . . to hell with everything," I repeated slowly as she squeezed my nipple harder. I pressed against her and closed my eyes. And the world went to hell.

The fact that the world is slowly going to hell is true in general too. Well, at least the world as I know it. On my way to work . . . on one of the ways to what I call work, my eyes fixed again on one of the many cafés. But this time I didn't sit down because I had no one to sit down with. I saw a monster. Let me be more specific: I saw a creature that's in my book of the world's biggest monstrosities and horrors. My gaze lingered, but only for a few tenths of a second, on a motley collection of beer bottles, bright red lips, butch-looking fake leather jackets, pagers, perms and mustaches—the rough shot you get in a few tenths of a second. I saw my ex-girlfriend, one of those I count among my ex-wives—someone who was once really important to me. And who now isn't even important to herself. But admittedly, I did spend a tenth of a second just taking in the picture of her. So. She was sitting with her legs splayed in her usual, mannish pose; her left hand was resting on her knee while her right hand was holding a cigarette, which, at that point, was on its way to her mouth that was turned up into a firm, self-satisfied smile. She wasn't talking.

I think she was nodding to the loud mustache sitting on the opposite side of the table. Her hair was longer—permed, with bright highlights. If that wasn't enough, she had plucked eyebrows, thinned down to ridiculous ornamental commas, and mascara on her eyelashes. There was no doubt about it: my ex had dressed up as a heterosexual and I'd never see what I considered the world with the same eyes again. When I saw that spectacle, I was overwhelmed with the kind of blunt pain I call the total or all-encompassing hurt of the world. The pain you sometimes feel when you see all those bullet-ridden and starved bodies on the news. But you know you'll never stop looking at them because it's such a common sight there's no room for all-out despair. Yet sometimes you still get the urge to grab your head and bang it against the floor. But there's no point. There's no point in organizing charity events for those who are starving or addicted, no point in writing eco-conscious articles. That's

why I couldn't bring myself to contribute my own drop in the
ocean; I couldn't allow my train of thought to veer into the safe
haven of local activism. Not even for a moment did I think that
what I had there—practically right before my eyes—was a living example of homophobia and the product of social pressure
or weak character. You can see it if you want to. You can write
about it if you feel like it. Or you can let it slip. Out of your
hands. Your mind. That's the global hurt that you can't put your
finger on. If some other woman saw her ex-husband acting like
the most stereotypical fag . . . Maybe she could go crying to
some Western gossip rag: "My Ex Has Gone Homo." My ex was
dressed up as a heterosexual woman.

Anyway, when I saw the pathetic spectacle with mascara on
her eyes that was my ex-wife, a woman who knew how to wear
a pair of jeans on her hips and lean up against a bar confidently,
I could no longer have a bad day. I was happy because I knew
Ana. And I knew myself.

My grandmother died when I was on vacation. I was too far
away to get back in time for her funeral. And because of that,
she's still turning in her grave. What else can she do? One of
my relatives called me and told me I was an heir—that's how I
found out my grandmother was dead. My first thought was that
I'd inherited the cesspool and that, thank God, I already knew
everything about it.

Yesterday I didn't go to work because I had two teeth out.
But it wasn't too bad; I learned some great news when I got
home—the Lustig Leben garden center came through and wired
the money by the deadline. With that money I could afford to
get more teeth fixed than I have. I went over to Ana's basement
room with bloody cotton pads in my mouth. I didn't phone her
because I couldn't talk. Ana was glad to see me. She made me
coffee and gave me a straw to drink through as I still couldn't
open my mouth properly.

"You know," she said, "I get lost sometimes. Every so often
when I get really high I don't know where I am for a few tenths

of a second. This one time, I was in Palma with a friend and at some point I had no idea what the fuck was going on. I didn't know where I was. I thought it was impossible, not knowing that, but it was true. At first I thought I was at my friend's place, but the space was too big and he lives in a studio apartment. Then I thought I was at Club K4, but everything was different. When I finally realized I was in Palma, I was terribly relieved I hadn't gone completely crazy just yet. But that happened to me at least three times that night. Well, at least I remembered the second time around that I did in fact know where I was and it was all a matter of getting into the right frame of mind to find out. And it was true—every single time I was relieved to discover I was in Palma!"

I was nodding, trying to smile, which was supposed to mean I understood what she was talking about. Sometimes I forget what I was just saying—usually when I'm really high. I don't know what I'm talking about and I have no idea what else I wanted to say to finish my thought. But it's not a big deal. I just stop talking and wait for it to come back to me. But sometimes I can't finish a story. I run out of material in the middle of a sentence and have to shut up. But because I had cotton pads in my mouth, I was quiet anyway and didn't have to explain all of this to Ana.

A few hours later we went out for a pizza. After that she took me up to the Ljubljana Castle. When it started to grow dark, we lighted a joint in the car. We could have gotten lost in our own thoughts, watching the lunar eclipse, but there wasn't one that night.

"You know," said Ana. "You know, I got a good paycheck from Lustig Leben. And now I don't know if I want to go back to school. I'm afraid I can't really do anything. Sometimes I feel like the only thing I can do is smoke pot and sell it. I know how to do that. Maybe I'll go to school; some other time . . . next year. But the money at Lustig Leben is really good. We don't have to have lunch with my parents anymore. Never again.

Maybe we could even go away for the weekend and stay at some B&B like the other normal people down there."

She pointed a finger at other normal people in Ljubljana who were now reduced to specks of light. I had to laugh. She was beautiful in the faint glow of the street lamps and almost any shirt she had on could have been red and checkered. I thought, it's good to know Ana, to go for a drive and get high with her.

"I wanted to tell you something earlier. When I had the cotton pads in my mouth and I couldn't talk. But now I can't remember what it was. By the way, I got paid too."

Ana laughed. She reached her hand under my T-shirt, running her fingers down my spine. And like so many times before, the world went to hell.

TRANSLATED BY ŠPELA BIBIČ

GEOGRAPHICAL POSITIONS

Studying maps has always been a very special and mysterious activity for me. The first secret is that you don't look at a map, you read it.

At an international conference for lesbian and gay rights, I shared a room with Krisa from Fiji. Never before had I even thought about what people from that island, which is its own country, looked like. Krisa was thin, had somewhat darker skin, and slightly slanted eyes. When I asked her the meaning of the drawings, apart from the sea motifs tattooed on her upper arm and forearm, she said they were Chinese characters. Her father was Chinese, her mother, Fijian. "If you think that the inhabitants of my island look like me, you're very mistaken," she explained to me. "They all have darker skin, more pronounced features and their eyes are straight, almost like you Europeans."

Reading, of course, is something you learn at school. Then you read a map and have to make out north and south, east and west. Why north should be up isn't entirely obvious and it's in fact only "up" on the map. In reality, the universe out there couldn't care less about up and down. But this is still okay. We know where south is, it's down after all and we all say that everyone "looks down" on southerners. According to this, we could "look up" to people from the north, but I'm not sure if it works this way or not. Fine, east and west—right and left. Right is east, that's where Russians and communism are; left is west, where Americans and other capitalists are. You can try to remember it all like this: on the right are communists, who are

politically left wing, and on the left are the capitalists, who are
politically right wing. This is more complicated, but I think it's
easier to remember. Of course, this also depends on your current
political situation. Nowadays left and right aren't what they used
to be. It used to be much easier to read maps, when we weren't
in transition. Just the fact that time has something to do with
all this is enough—on some points on a map, it can be an hour
later or earlier than somewhere else—especially if you're looking
at it all from some sort of transition.

Before using logic, one has to learn a bunch of facts that
don't seem to go together. It just doesn't seem logical that east
is east, so you need something else to remember its position. For
example, that east is on the right side or that it is communist
or backward or that it reeks of garlic (even Dracula, for whom
garlic is a repellant, comes from the east). You get the feeling
that you've been cheating learning all these positions. That's
why I sometimes worry what my (geographical) logic is based
on. I'm afraid that it's still based on cheating. If I hear that a
certain place is in the east, of course I know where east is, but
at the same time, I think to myself that I have to read the right
side of the map. To the right of Europe.

Two days later when Krisa and I were hugging each other in
bed, we first had to come to an agreement about geographical
positions. She didn't know where Slovenia was and asked me if
English was our only official language. I told her that we spoke
Slovene, but there really wasn't much point to that because she
could only understand Slovenia as being a part of Europe—this
was probably her way of cheating when learning about places
outside of Oceania. Though, I wasn't much better—I couldn't
place Fiji on that map in my head. I kept getting lost, I wasn't
able to place it on the left or the right. When I was back home, I
finally looked at a map of the world; I usually looked for Oceania
on the right side. And so I began my search for Krisa's island. I
looked to the extreme right and found Fiji. Then I looked to the

extreme left and found Fiji there too!

Krisa had had more than enough of her island of Fiji. She wanted to go to America, to New York, San Francisco, anywhere. She knew very little about Europe and that the continent seemed too foreign. My explanations about Europe being called the Old World as opposed to America being called the New World were a waste of time. She said she seemed to have once heard something about this, but my explanations were too abstract for her, perhaps even unreal. Krisa wanted to study in America. At home she worked for a non-governmental organization for sexual minorities, which in the eyes of the locals wasn't worthy of respect. My Fijian roommate had many problems with respect in general. Now that she'd finally got a job and moved into an apartment with her three children, everyone found out that she was a no-good lesbian, even though she herself categorized herself as bisexual.

Before that she'd been without her kids for some months because she'd left home. She left home because her brother had beaten her unconscious. He beat her up because she'd told him that a taxi driver had raped her. The taxi driver had raped her because her friend had gotten out of the taxi before her and Krisa had been left alone with the driver. They had taken a taxi because they'd been going home very late at night, or morning rather, at six when it was still dark and too dangerous to go on foot. They'd been so late because Krisa had been working as a DJ in a club, her friend as a waitress.

So, to the right and to the left of Europe—there's Fiji times two—at least for me. For Krisa there was no Slovenia and probably only one Fiji. Surely she doesn't read maps on the "left and right sides" of Europe. Europe is the center of the map to me, the point I don't search left or right for, up or down. This centered view of Europe pushes other territories to the extreme edges of paper maps. What about a round globe on which all places are the same? Reading a globe isn't as pleasant for an eye that isn't used to it. Its center is somewhere else—somewhere deep down in the magma, but no less geo/egocentric.

One evening after a busy day at the conference, three of us got together in the room and were drinking wine. Krisa combed her long hair in front of the mirror, Esthera from Latvia and I had wrapped ourselves in cigarette smoke.

"Then I remembered that it had begun even earlier," Krisa suddenly said in the bathroom.

Esthera and I looked at each other and waited for Krisa to go on. After the rape and her brother's beatings, she left home and left her kids with her mother. She was no longer able to work as a DJ, so she rented a room and began to earn money as a prostitute.

"It's a long way from the best profession in the world," she said as she came out of the bathroom with her shiny blue hair combed, "Yet I found it very informative."

She laughed sharply and the two of us joined her with careful smiles. We'd noticed that she often laughed at inappropriate times. She sat down with us, drank some wine and then continued.

Most of the time, I probably still imagine the world in a primitive way: flat. My favorite cartographic projection.

Whenever I fly from one town to another, I never think about how much of the earth's curved surface is between them. Distances on a flat map seem friendlier to me somehow, shorter, easier to conquer.

While prostituting she realized that there'd been others before the taxi driver. She'd been raped by her older brother, the one who beat her up for getting raped. And before that by her uncle, who'd never let her leave the table until she'd eaten everything up. When her clients paid her for sex, she finally remembered why she had such unpleasant memories of the part of her childhood she'd spent at her uncle's while her parents had been in China. Perhaps she'd forgotten about it because she'd known that she wouldn't have been able to tell anyone. Rather, no one would've believed her.

There are, of course, measurements for geographical coordinates. They're usually found in the lower right-hand corner of most maps.

"But sometimes it's possible," the Latvian said pensively. Krisa and I looked at her in surprise. "Sometimes it's possible," she continued, "for an adult to love a child. I mean: like a sexual object."

"But that's abuse," Krisa and I said in unison. "It's always abuse, everywhere. A child isn't responsible for itself, an adult is. A child doesn't have all the information, an adult knows what he or she is doing."

"I know," said the Latvian quietly. "But still. A child can also love an adult. You love and desire without information and responsibility. I'm only saying that it's possible."

A shadow of disappointment and rage covered Krisa's face as she drank down what was left in her glass.

"Perhaps it's possible," she said with a blunt look centered at the hotel wallpaper above Esthera's head, "but that's deception. Manipulation."

"And love between two adults is never deceitful?" Esthera asked.

I shrugged, "I think that's beside the point."

"Whatever, I don't know anything about love between adults and children," said Krisa as she laughed sharply. This time her laughter had cut the conversation. And all three of us silently tried to regain our balance on the slippery terrain on which we'd found ourselves.

Without numbers that express ratios, one to so much and so many thousands, tens of thousands or hundreds of thousands, we'd find it hard to believe that we actually read anything on a map.

Then Krisa thought that we could still go for some

champagne, it was after all our last evening together. We quickly got dressed and left the window open.

In the hotel lobby I looked at a local map. We were all at the same point: 26 degrees south and 29 degrees east.

TRANSLATED BY ELIZABETA ŽARGI, REVISED BY KELLY LENOX

SOMETHING I'VE NEVER UNDERSTOOD
ABOUT TAKING THE TRAIN

"That's why we have to get to the hospital in Ljubljana. But there's no time for that, don't you see? There's so much to do at home," the woman sitting across from me says. I nod and say nothing, hoping she'll lose interest in talking to me. It's not even seven a.m. yet. I've never understood people who are so chatty first thing in the morning. Much less people who seem so enthusiastic about striking up conversations with strangers on trains.

The rumble home by train once every month, followed the next Monday morning by the return trip to Ljubljana, has always put me in mind of a journey into exile. Every time I boarded the train to Ljubljana at 5:25 a.m. and found my seat, I wanted to seal off the compartment. Or have my own separate train car. Since, however, that wasn't possible, I'd at least wish for quiet, sleepy travel companions capable of nothing more than a grunt before nine a.m., who didn't torture their fellows by forcing conversations on them. Of course, I was almost never that lucky, and this day least of all. As early as Beltinci, three extraordinarily alert women entered my compartment—an old woman, her daughter-in-law, and her sister. The one who explains to me tirelessly that her mother-in-law has some strange growth on her back is the daughter-in-law, an unbearably practical woman. In the same breath she also manages to tell me that the tomatoes have been terrible this year, that most of them are still green and that she's going to have to pick all the green ones and put them away for the winter. She's not sure if she'll manage it, since now she's going to have to spend two days in Ljubljana until her mother-in-law has her operation, and in the meantime a hailstorm could wipe out everything. Whenever you leave, that's when the hail chooses to strike. But her mother-in-law insisted on having her operation in Ljubljana, because that's where the best doctors are. "This is true," I said, nodding. "Yes, of course it's true," said the daughter-in-law testily, "if you're young. But when you reach eighty-five like her, things are different. She's old enough as it is and she's going to have die of something. But she insists she wants to get well. So what can you do?" The mother-in-law laughed riotously and even I had to smile, though I don't quite know why. Then she took a sandwich filled with fat, greasy slabs of salami and shoved it at her mother-in-law, "What's the problem, Mother? Have a sandwich." The old woman laughed and said she'd already eaten at home. Then the daughter-in-law offered the sandwich to me, but I declined, my stomach turning from the stench of the salami. Then the old woman's sister, thank God, complained she was cold and the three women went in search of a warmer compartment. They invited me to join them, but I explained that I preferred it cool.

Relieved, I kicked my shoes off and stretched my legs out onto the seat across from me. Barely had I managed to get my eyes properly shut than the train stopped at Ptuj and hordes of high school brats mobbed the compartments. They're also big on noisily talking, swearing, chewing their sandwiches and endlessly lighting up cigarettes first thing in the morning. Three boys and an older man came into my compartment, the man being someone the boys knew, but otherwise a migrant laborer. I decided to keep my eyes closed. When they sat down they began whispering something to each other and guffawing. I pulled my coat up over me and turned my face to the window, leaving as little of me as possible exposed to their intrusive stares. "What is that, a dude or a chick?" the older man asks in a half-whisper. The boys guffaw. Through the slits of my eyelids I can see one of the boys making hand gestures—apparently trying to show that he can see my tits, so I must be a chick. I have no idea how he can see them through the winter coat that covers me like a blanket. Then they start talking more loudly. It's obvious they'd normally be talking to each other in an ordinary tone of voice, but their ill-concealed remarks are directed mostly at me. To the effect, for instance, that they should wake me up, since a woman snoozing like this at eight in the morning mustn't be good for much. Maybe they can invite me for coffee and a smoke. If I'm not married, that is. "She isn't, she isn't," one of the more pimply brats announced, "There's no ring on her finger." That was another thing I've never understood—how people could be so focused on the presence or absence of wedding rings on other people's hands, especially kids this age. At least now I'd know for next time—just to be safe—to wear a ring, and maybe then people would give me a little more peace, if they thought I was married.

But for the time being I was rescued by a grumpy conductor. After checking our tickets, he laid into the boys, "This is a non-smoking car." And turning to the man he said, "You, sir, could at least set an example for them and keep your grimy shoes off the seats." The man muttered something and winked at the boys, who were grinning and elbowing each other in the ribs. Shaking his head, the dismayed conductor slammed the door shut behind him. By then we'd already reached Pragersko, where a restaurant car gets attached to the train, and all of them were off for a beer.

After that I had an hour's peace. During that time for some mysterious reason the train stopped for a half hour, but I had no interest in looking out the window. I heard a lot of talking and anxious footsteps outside the window of my compartment and somebody shouted a few times that there'd just been an accident. Some woman—I'll bet it was the daughter-in-law who was taking her mother-in-law to the hospital in Ljubljana—said that there was a bloody mess on the tracks, but that at least the forecast was for rain that afternoon. I had not the slightest wish to open the window and sate my curiosity so early in the morning by watching all the stunned people milling around. Frankly, I've never understood people who have the habit of running out into the street, even in the middle of the night and in just their pajamas, to see a car wreck or some mangled corpse or a pool of blood, at the very least. And if I were ever in such an accident, I sincerely hope nobody comes out to gawk at me and guess if my body is a man's or a woman's, or if I'm too young to have died, or look for the wedding ring on my finger.

I slept soundly for a short while. I was woken by the compartment door opening: a man of indeterminate age came in. His face was sweaty and pale, or maybe he was just that sleepy. He pointed inquiringly at the seat by the door. I nodded. He smiled briefly and sat down. He sat still wearing his overcoat, even though it had become quite warm in the compartment. His coat was filthy with mud and some dark stain and his hands were black, as though he'd been digging through dirt with them. When he noticed me looking at his hands, he quickly hid them in his pockets and smiled in embarrassment. I smiled back, also embarrassed. I felt as though one or the other of us ought to say something. "Did you see the accident? What happened?" I asked, even though I wasn't really curious. "Yes and no," he said. "What was it?" I asked him again. "Oh, I'm so tired," he said absently. "Sometimes you just can't go on any longer. It'd be hard for me to say just what went wrong in my life, I'm no psychologist, nothing of the sort, really. I have a house and a garden that year after year bears a ton of unripe vegetables, I have a wife who'd do anything for others, why she even looks after her deaf mother-in-law and her greedy aunt more than she does me." He sniveled and fell silent. I was getting nervous. You see, I've never been able to understand how some people can cry in public, in the presence of perfect strangers. Still, it seemed like I ought to say something to him. But I'm no good at these things. So I cleared my throat and stupidly asked him, "Do you have any children? Don't they care?" The man shook his head vehemently. "Children? I have three shameless, pimply brats, all of them worthless for work or book-learning. They look up to my shiftless brother, who provides them with a constant supply of beer and stupid pranks. Would you call those children?" This gave me pause, but only because I was at a loss again for the right words to comfort him. "Well, I suppose," I started off shakily, "though I don't have experience with children, myself . . . but eventually they do grow up, you know, and they won't always be so . . . like that." He opened his mouth, but then he clutched his side in a sudden bolt of pain. "Young lady," he grimaced and went on, "that's exactly what I don't want to see happen. I don't want anyone to grow up and get old and all the rest of it. I don't want things to go on! I can't understand where they find the taste for it. At eighty-five my mother can't wait to have her next operation. They'd do anything to keep things from changing! Now what would you do in my place?" I shook my head. I honestly wouldn't know what to do in his place. So he told me. He told me that one day—if I were in his place, of course—one day, when my wife, mother, and aunt had taken off for Ljubljana, and my brats had gone with my shiftless brother to school, I'd throw myself under an oncoming train. But since I'm not in his place, I don't have to do that. But he's in his place and that's what he's done—for an instant he opened his coat to show me his butchered side, wheezing *I beg your pardon*—and he's completely baffled how that damn train managed to brake so fast. And then all those conductors and track inspectors and signalmen came running, and none of them could've given a shit what became of their work as a result. Then there were the passengers sticking their heads out the windows and turning away in disgust, but then they got their relatives, friends, acquaintances, and total strangers to come and gape, too. "You see, I was in such a bad way, and I still am now. So much of me is missing, but still I'm alive, and still thinking, and all of it just keeps on going. All of them looked at my body and said what a poor bastard, what an idiot, think of his poor children, if he has any, and his poor wife, who'll be all alone."

Thank goodness we were already approaching Ljubljana and I'd be getting off soon, as I was already starting to feel responsible for him. As the train raced past Ljubljana–Polje I was able to ask him, more casually now, "I suppose now you'll head to the hospital?" But he told me that he'd quit going to hospitals, because he couldn't bear all the visitors who came to gawk. "Now tell me, would you go to a hospital—if you were in my place, of course?" "I really don't know," I said frankly. "Well, if I were in my place I wouldn't, and I won't," he said mournfully. "Why else do you suppose I got up and crawled under the train cars? So they wouldn't find me. And got on the train? I'm not going back home."

The train came to a stop at the Ljubljana main station. I pulled down my suitcase and put on my coat. "I'm getting off here," I said. He nodded. I could tell he was looking forward to being alone. "Well, I'm off," I said, once more somewhat awkwardly. "Could I ask you a favor?" he said plaintively. "Sure, name it," I said, already standing in the doorway. "Leave me the newspaper."

TRANSLATED BY MICHAEL BIGGINS

Suzana Tratnik (born 1963) is a writer, translator, publicist, and sociologist. She has published six short-story collections, two novels (*My Name is Damjan* and *Third World*), a play, and three works of nonfiction. Tratnik was one of the founders of the LGBT-rights movement in 1980s Yugoslavia and was instrumental in creating one of Eastern Europe's most vibrant alternative cultural scenes before the fall of the Berlin Wall. In 2007 she was awarded the Prešeren Foundation Prize, one of Slovenia's most prestigious literary awards.

Michael Biggins's translations of works by Slovene authors such as Drago Jančar, Tomaž Šalamun, Vladimir Bartol, and Lojze Kovačič have been published by Harcourt, Archipelago, and Dalkey Archive, among others. In 2015 he was awarded the Lavrin Diploma of the Society of Slovene Literary Translators for distinguished contributions to the advancement of Slovene literature in English. He lives in Seattle.

Špela Bibič (1986) holds a degree in Translation Studies (English-French) and works as a freelance translator. To date, she has translated two novels into Slovenian – Renée Vivien's Une femme m'apparut (ŠKUC, 2011) and Georges Eekhoud's Escal-Vigor (ŠKUC, 2012). Her English translations of short fiction by prominent Slovenian authors have appeared in a number of anthologies and other publications.

Mojka Šoštarko is a literary translator and critic. She currently lives in Ljubljana, Slovenia.

Elizabeta Žargi was born and bred in Montreal, Canada to a Slovenia father and Scottish-Canadian mother. She currently teaches English Language and Literature in Amman, Jordan. Published translations include *Banalities* by Brane Mozetič (2008).